RAIN FALL

Also by Ella West

Night Vision

To Bob,
who taught me how to ride a horse

◆ ◆ ◆

Westport, the town where I live, lies (mostly) between the banks of the Buller and Orowaiti rivers. The Buller flows fast and deep through bush and gorges. It finally emerges amid a narrow strip of farmland before being channelled to the sea at the south end of the town between two man-made tip heads. After running freely from wild mountains deep inland, I think it must be embarrassed when it becomes a river port and then, even worse, has its final send-off over the dredged river bar into the Tasman. It gets its revenge, however, because when it rains the Buller swells to be the largest river in New Zealand and then nothing stands in its way. It tears whole trees from its banks, will take farmland and close roads. Nothing survives if caught in its waters.

The Orowaiti River, to the north, takes a much shorter trip to the sea, draining only some swamps and tidal zones before meandering through a muddy estuary, which they call a lagoon, before it splashes into the surf at Fairdown Beach. When in flood, the Buller pushes its way into the Orowaiti's waters and surrounds Westport. Then both rivers are bank to bank, only centimetres from the bottom of their road and rail bridges. I've seen it like that several times.

But there's been no rain for weeks and today, Saturday morning, the Orowaiti is quiet, the tide flowing out far beneath the road bridge as I cycle over it on my way to basketball practice in town. I live on Utopia Road (and no it's not, in case you're wondering) and it's only about a ten-minute bike ride through dairy farms and the cemetery, across the Orowaiti Bridge and past all the houses on Brougham Street to Domett Street and the indoor basketball courts next to the swimming pool.

And today I'm not running late, like I usually am. Maybe that's why I look in the river, see the grey sky reflected in the grey water. Maybe that's why I stop, then ride over to the other side to watch it emerge again from under the bridge. It's a coat. Floating. A dark-coloured coat, the sleeves spread wide, heading hood-first down the river.

And then it starts to rain.

1

In other languages there are a million zillion words for snow or ice or heat. In English it's words for rain – drizzle, mist, trickle, sprinkle, fog, shower, cloudburst, downpour, deluge, torrent, storm, flood and a whole lot more that I can't think of right now. And here, in Westport, we measure rain not in centimetres but in metres. Two, or maybe three. In a bad year we can have more. It can rain so much and for so long that the grass turns yellow, doors become swollen and then stick, paper won't go through photocopiers or printers and people draw pictures of the sun and sticky-tape them to the windows at their workplaces and at school as a joke. Just so no one forgets what the sun looks like.

Even if you wear a coat or use an umbrella it won't stop you getting wet. This rain doesn't just fall. It wraps itself around you, you breathe it in, the whole world becomes water, constant falling water. And we drag it inside with us. Small rivers run off our clothes and our shoes onto the floor as we sit in class, wet hair pushed behind ears, steam rising off our shoulders. A wet fug. At home the fire is always going – usually not because it's cold, but to try to keep the house dry. No use having a dehumidifier. There's no way to dry out the house and everything wet from outside as well. So our ceilings grow mould. Black patterns creep across them until Mum, grumbling, wipes them off with a cloth soaked in bleach.

When it rains, the only difference between the days is the size of the drops and the time it takes for them to fall.

And once it starts it doesn't stop.

When the fine drizzle suddenly becomes a cloudburst you can hear it coming. It reaches the bush first, the rain hitting each leaf before falling to the ground, the noise like a thousand deer racing towards you. And then there is the continuous sound of it on the windscreen when you're in the car, on the school roof during the day, at home afterwards. You listen to it lying in bed at night when you're trying to get to sleep, and it's still there when you wake up in the morning. It drums on your head as you walk or run or bike. Each drop hitting you, splashing on you, the sound, the noise. Sometimes you just wish for quiet. For it to be quiet. For the rain to just shut up.

But it won't.

It controls your life, what you do, how you do it. Outside sports are cancelled, Guy Fawkes and beach parties planned weeks in advance are washed out. And there's nothing to do. There are no shopping malls, no places to go, no inside stuff. You just sit there by the window, watching the rain fall.

Mum usually drives me to and from school on her way to work, especially when it's raining. She runs the office at St Canice's, the Catholic primary school, not that she's Catholic. But then, nor are most of the kids who go there. Well, not churchgoing Catholics, obey the scriptures, do no evil and all that, or so she says to Dad. I went to North School, one of the other two primary schools in town (the third has the equally original name of South School) before going to Buller High where it doesn't matter whether you're Catholic or not. You're all just the same. You are all just nobodies.

But today I don't want Mum to drive me. Today I am rebelling. After almost a week of rain I need some fresh air, even if it will be mostly wet fresh air. There's a basketball game at lunchtime against Kaiapoi High. It's a school interchange, the Canterbury high school playing us in everything both schools can put teams together for. And they're better

5

than us in most of them – except for basketball. We have to win, so I want to get my head straight, which means not having Mum talk to me about her problems all the way to school in the car in the hope that I will then share all mine with her. Today I have one problem only: win the game for my team, for my school. And that is it.

We should win okay. I've been dropping a few three-pointers lately, getting good at them. A few of those, and the scoreboard climbs. As long as I get fed the ball we can do it.

I find my bike in the carport at the back of the house and start pedalling. Just out of the driveway the wind blows back my hood and it's about then that I start to question my decision. I push the pedals harder and squint through the rivers of water already running off my hair and into my eyes. A grey car is parked on the side of the road, which is unusual. Cars don't usually park along here. There's no reason for them to park along here.

The driver's door opens and a man gets out. He holds up his hand to stop me as I approach. He's got a black parka on, black pants, black leather shoes. His hair is getting wet. I put one foot on the ground, the other still on the pedal just in case.

'You can't pass through here,' he says.

'Why not?'

'You've got to get off the road now.'

'I've got to get to school.'

'Not today, you don't. Where do you live?'

I point out our driveway.

'You bike back and I'll follow. Quickly.'

Some adults you don't question. This guy seems to be one of them. I cycle back home and he follows me in his car, staying drier than I do.

I leave my bike against the side of the house and climb the three steps to our porch and open the front door. The man is right behind me.

'Mum, Dad, there's someone here to see you,' I call down the hallway. Dad has just come off shift. I don't think he'll have gone to bed yet.

'What's that, Annie? Why aren't you on your way to school?' Mum yells from the kitchen. 'I thought you were biking. Have you changed your mind? Do you want a lift now?'

Dad, still in his orange and blue overalls with their reflective stripes, pops his head and shoulders into the hallway from the living room. I can just hear *Breakfast* on the TV. Then Dad sees the man standing behind me, in the front doorway.

'Sir,' the mystery man says, stepping into the hallway and closing the door behind him, 'I need you all to stay inside for the next few hours and keep away from your front windows.'

'Why, what's going on?' Dad asks, walking down the hallway towards us. The TV suddenly goes quiet. Mum must have turned it off.

'Detective Wilson, up from Greymouth.'

They shake hands.

'What's going on? Has Annie done something?'

'Dad, I need to get to school.'

'Just a minute, pet.'

'I've got basketball. Against Kaiapoi.'

'What's all this?' Mum asks, drying her hands on a tea towel she has for some reason brought into the hallway with her to meet a stranger.

'This man is a cop from Greymouth,' Dad says.

'Annie?'

'There is an incident occurring across the road just along from here and your house is in line of sight, as is the road,' the detective says.

'You mean the O'Shea house?' Mum asks.

'A man known to police fired a gun in town last night and we believe he is now in the house across from you.'

'It must be the O'Shea house, that's the only one. The box-shaped house with no garden?'

'You mean Pete did this?' Dad asks, frowning.

'I can't say.'

'His mum died a few months back. Pete wouldn't do anything.'

'Dad, tell him I need to get to school.'

'So how long is this going to go on for?'

'At least the morning. We think he's sleeping it off for now.'

'So we can't go outside all morning, we can't leave?' Mum asks. 'I've got to get to work.'

'There will be nothing going along this road until this is over. We're putting roadblocks in place at the moment. I need you all to stay inside, away from the windows. You'll do that?'

Dad nods.

'I don't want any of you becoming a target. I should evacuate you all.'

'That's not Pete,' Mum says, shaking her head.

'Doesn't sound like the Pete we know,' Dad says.

'He narrowly missed shooting someone through the window in the police station last night.'

My parents exchange glances. In the silence Detective Wilson decides to leave, probably because he realises he's in the middle of an argument he can't win. He's from Greymouth; my parents are Pete's neighbours. Of course they know Pete better than he does. Dad shuts the door behind Detective Wilson, after taking a second to glance outside.

'Anything?' Mum asks.

'Nothing. They've got him mixed up with someone else. Pete wouldn't do anything that dumb.' He yawns. 'Anyway, I'm going to bed.'

'I'd better ring work,' Mum says to me. 'And your school.'

They both head back to the other end of the house leaving me standing there, still dripping on the floor from the rain, my schoolbag with my basketball shoes and shorts inside at my feet.

2

I sit on the end of my bed and stare out across the room through the window at the O'Shea house. I can't see a lot, in the rain. It's steady at the moment, a curtain of grey. I can see our lawn and our low hedge, then across Utopia Road, and over to the far right I can just make out the corner of the O'Shea house in the gloom. It's yellow. Not bright yellow but a dull, faded yellow, almost cream. Some of the boards look rotten and the roof has a tilt to one corner like it's going to slide right off the house one day. This house is just a box, nothing likeable about it. In front of it, along the path, someone once placed grey bricks on an angle as a garden border, not that there are any plants. I've always thought the bricks look like jagged teeth.

11

Nothing seems to be happening. There are no cars or trucks moving on the road, everything is quiet. Sitting on my bed I should be far enough away from the window that no one can see me. I can't see anything through the O'Shea house's windows. No Pete with a gun pointed at me, anyway. Not that he would do that. His mum, her name was Mary, used to come over and babysit me when I was little. Sometimes he would come as well, play with my toys with me. And he would always be waiting for the school bus when I used to take it before Mum got the job at St Canice's, before I was big enough to bike into town. Most of the time he would talk to the other older guys but he always said hello, or smiled at me, acknowledged in some way that I was there. I remember him grabbing me once when I thought it was a good idea to run in front of the stopped bus to cross the road. There was a car coming and I hadn't seen it because the bus was in the way. He probably saved my life that day. I don't know. I was too young to understand, and too young to thank him. I just remember being angry because when he had grabbed me, he'd hurt my arm. He must have said something to his mum, and his mum had said something to my mum, because I got a telling-off that night. Afterwards, though, I always waited for the bus to go before crossing the road. And I never ran.

But it was a long time ago now. I haven't seen Pete for months, maybe a year. He would be eighteen or nineteen now. He's left school, I know that – he's not at Buller High anymore – but I don't know what he does these days. He's probably unemployed, like most people around here. Mary died a couple of months ago – heart attack, but she had been ill for ages. Mum used to take the odd meal over, to help out, but she hasn't done it since the funeral. I suppose Pete inherited the house; it must be kind of weird, owning your own home when you're not even twenty, being responsible. But then, where else would he go? He's always lived there with his mum, just the two of them, and now there'll be just him. There's never been a dad, or brothers or sisters. I think they had a dog. I've sometimes heard a dog there, barking inside the house. But not lately. Maybe it's died too.

Sleeping it off, the detective said. Sleeping off what, I wonder. Drugs? Booze? Both? If Pete's asleep, why don't they just go in and take him? I doubt he locks his doors. We don't. The front door when we go out, but never the back door. No one does. This is Westport. And even if Pete has locked all the doors, there are windows and a million ways to get in – either quietly so as not to wake him or they could bash the door down, break a window, throw in tear gas. They are the police. Not that they need to do any of those things. It's just *Pete*.

Dad is snoring in his bedroom across the hallway. I can just hear him over the noise of the rain. He must think his bed is far enough away from the windows too, or he doesn't care. Pete would never do something like that, he said. And he's right.

I check my phone again. Almost ten. Two and a half hours to the basketball game.

I could sneak out, jump the fences in the paddocks behind our house before circling around onto the road. But then I wouldn't have my bike and it would be a long walk to school. And my mum wouldn't let me do it, and if I didn't tell her she'd freak when she found out I was gone, and I'd never hear the end of it. I'm stuck here until it's over.

I should study or read or turn on my laptop or go see Blue, my horse, or something – but I keep sitting here, watching.

'Hey, you, I thought you might like a hot chocolate.'

Mum is at my bedroom doorway, holding out a mug. I reach to take it and she sits next to me on the end of the bed. She has a cup of coffee. She hasn't changed out of her work clothes, just like I'm still in my school uniform. We both look out of the window.

'When is the basketball game?'

'Lunchtime.'

'Twelve-thirty?'

I nod and take a sip from the mug. My mum knows what a good hot chocolate is. We've got one of those machines with the capsules. She says it makes a good coffee too.

'What's going on out there?' she asks.

'Nothing much,' I say, my face still over my mug.

'Take a look now.'

I glance up at the window. I can see rain, lawn, hedge, road and figures in black coming out from behind trees and fences.

'They weren't there before.'

'It'll be the Armed Offenders Squad up from Greymouth.'

'They look kind of ridiculous.'

I can make out helmets, vests, backpacks, everything black. One of the figures is running between the others, handing out something, talking to each of them.

'What are they doing?' I ask.

'I can't believe it.' Mum laughs. 'That guy is handing out morning tea to them all. See, brown paper bags. Probably mince pies from Freckles.'

We watch as the figures put down their weapons and eat whatever is in the paper bags. Take sips from takeaway coffee cups. They're in clusters. There is nodding, glances around as if they're talking about the weather, their plans for the weekend, how good the pies are, which they are – Freckles makes the best pies. A few of the glances are towards our house.

'Do you think they can see us?'

'No. We're far enough away from your window. If you turned the light on maybe they could.'

'What's going to happen?'

'Pete will wake up and wander out and they'll arrest him, I suppose.'

'Will he be okay?'

'I hope so. We'll make sure he gets a good lawyer. We owe that to Mary at the very least.'

'Is it going to be on TV?'

'Maybe. The news crew are probably having morning tea too. Maybe we should ring up Pete and tell him now is the time for him to go for it, everyone is scoffing mince pies.'

'Have you talked to him lately?'

'No. Not really. Not since the funeral. I'm not even sure if the phone is still connected. He might not be paying the bill. I haven't got his cell phone number.'

We're silent again, sipping our hot drinks, watching the cops eat their pies, thinking about Pete.

'They won't shoot him, will they?'

'Only if he comes out pointing a gun at them. Then they might. But he's not that stupid.'

'And if he is?'

'Just don't watch.' She laughs. 'Anyway, haven't you got homework or something to do? I don't know, Instagram or Facebook or whatever?'

'Everyone's in class.'

'Well, work was going to email me some stuff, so I suppose I'd better go and do it. Stay away from the window, won't you? Remember what that detective said.'

I nod again, still holding the mug in both hands, still staring out of the window at the rain as she leaves.

Dad is still snoring too.

Morning tea eaten, the Armed Offenders Squad melt back into their hiding places. Now I know they're there, I can make them out, just. Will Pete know they're there? Have the cops already rung him, if they know his phone number? Maybe we should give it to them. If he has paid his phone bill. Maybe his mum paid it months in advance before she died, knowing that he wouldn't get around to it, along with the power and the rates and the Sky TV subscription. A satellite dish has been on the house's roof for as long as I can remember, before you had to have one when TV turned over to digital, so I think he has Sky, or did have Sky. Maybe the cops are bargaining with him on the phone right now, *come out with no weapons and we won't shoot you*, Pete wanting them just to go away and leave him alone, or demanding a plane and a bag of money. Or maybe they're still waiting for him to sleep it off, whatever that means. Maybe he's watching sport on Sky.

Two hours to the basketball game.

Still raining.

Thomas, our cat, comes into my room squawking. He jumps up onto the bed and purrs louder than Dad's snoring, demanding to be patted, scratched under the chin, between his ears. Then he jumps off again and sticks his head into my hot chocolate mug, which is now on the floor, and starts licking at the remains. I swat him away and he saunters out of the room, his tail in the air, as if he hasn't done anything wrong.

One and three-quarter hours to the basketball game.

Outside there's movement – no, there isn't. Am I imagining it? Grey on grey, black shapes against green. No, there's nothing. All quiet and still. Except for the rain.

One hour and three minutes to the basketball game.

Mum hangs her head around my doorway. 'If this is over soon enough I'll take you to school,' she says.

I nod.

'It's only Kaiapoi,' she says.

'We've got to win, Mum.'

'I know, but there's always next year and anyway, maybe they'll win without you. It is a team sport, remember.'

I don't say anything. She leaves.

Fifty-two minutes to the basketball game.

Dad snoring.

How long does Pete have to sleep for? Is he snoring too? Like Dad? Have the cops got some listening device up against the wall of the house so they can hear him, so they know he's still asleep? If they have, I can't see it. I can't see anything in the rain.

Thirty-eight minutes to the basketball game.

It's a five-minute ride to school, if there isn't a milk tanker or something on the road in the way. Two minutes to run to the gym. I can get changed in the car. Put my gym shoes on when I get inside, so they're not wet.

There's movement out there again. Someone is going from group to group, heads together. Maybe they're putting in their lunch order, or maybe they're getting ready to go in, wake him up. Please, wake him up.

Fourteen minutes to the basketball game.

'Do you want some lunch?' Mum is at the door again. 'Toasted sandwich? I can do cheese, ham and pineapple.'

There's a flash of light and then noise and the feeling of someone punching me in the chest. Mum screams. I turn to the window and watch Pete's house explode in the rain.

3

Pete blew his house up with Powergel. It's all in *The Westport News*, the local newspaper, that afternoon. The police think it was with a timer or some sort of remote detonator (he could have used his phone) but they're not sure. They're not sure because they don't know if he was in the house or not when it blew up. They're not sure because there's nothing left. Maybe Pete set up the Powergel as some sort of booby-trap and it exploded by accident while he was still in there. Or maybe he wanted to blow himself up, but I hope not. Powergel is putty-like stuff in sausage-shaped tubes. They use it up at the mines for blasting. Dad says it's pretty safe to handle. You need a detonator to blow it up, and electricity; a battery will do it. At the mines they wire it and then the siren goes so everyone knows to get clear and then they push a button and *boom*. There was no siren when Pete used it on his house. There were plenty afterwards.

No one else is killed or hurt. Probably some of the Armed Offenders Squad can't hear afterwards for a bit, and the glass in my bedroom window and Mum and Dad's bedroom window is shattered. The explosion woke Dad up. He's not impressed.

No one seems to know how Pete got his hands on the Powergel. He wasn't working at the mines. The company that supplies it keeps it in a locked shed out on a pakihi terrace in the middle of nowhere – which is probably a good idea if you think about it, because if something does go wrong and it all blows up there are no houses close by. Maybe a weka or a few pukekoes would die, but that would be it. They probably wouldn't even find the feathers. Anyway, straight after the explosion they did a stocktake of the shed's contents and there was a lot of Powergel missing, far more than it had taken to blow up Pete's house. But that was nothing unusual, Dad said. Powergel goes missing all the time from that shed. It might be in the middle of nowhere, but everyone knows exactly where it is, and there's no one around to see anyone sneak up and break in and steal some. Makes you think, though – where is all that missing explosive?

I don't get to the basketball game and yes, we lose. Actually, we lose the whole interchange. Every team. The road outside is blocked with fire engines and police cars and even a helicopter hovers above us and it takes Mum a while to stop screaming and I have to pick the bits of glass out of my hair, so it's a lost cause. If Pete blew up his house two hours earlier I might have made it, but twelve minutes is pushing it. Mum rings up my school and explains what's happened and that I won't be there for the afternoon, which she doesn't really have to because not only is it in *The Westport News* but it's on TV at night and all over the internet so everyone knows about it, everyone in the whole world.

Dad says only something like this could happen in Westport, which makes me feel a little better. Where else in New Zealand does your neighbour blow up their house with Powergel when it's surrounded by Armed Offenders Squad members busy figuring out what to order for lunch? I do feel sad for Pete though. Not that we're sure he's dead, but if he isn't dead he has no house now, and it's where he grew up and where his mum died and there must have been a lot of memories for him there. It's also made a bit of a black wasteland across the road from us. After the explosion, what was left of the house caught fire and even the rain and the two Westport Volunteer Fire Brigade's engines couldn't put it out in time, so it burnt to the ground. I hope his dog, if he still had a dog, wasn't inside.

As Dad puts up tarpaulins over the broken windows to keep out the rain until the glazier can get to us, I pick up the bigger pieces of glass and Mum vacuums the floor in my bedroom and theirs. A TV news crew knocks on our front door to ask if we filmed the blast on our phones. Mum tells the reporter what she thinks about that. *Have you ever been this close to an explosion? Do you think getting our phones out to capture it was what we were thinking about at the time?* Dad stands in the hallway listening to her and laughs.

While they're talking to the reporter I slip out the back door to check on Blue, my horse. I want to make sure he's okay. I've started getting the shakes, I suppose from the explosion, and I need to get away from Mum and Dad fussing. Blue is my perfect excuse. As soon as he sees me he whinnies and walks over to the fence that separates his paddock from our back lawn. He wants his daily slab of hay, of course. If he's upset by the explosion and everything else, he doesn't show it. Food is more important to him than what we stupid people get up to, even if it is blowing up a house. I go into the shed to get the hay, retying the string on the bale in a loose bow, then shut the door behind me. I chuck the slab at him, bits of hay flying everywhere, and he takes a step back to reach down to where it has landed in the paddock, snorting through his nose as he does. His real name, his racing name, is something Country Blues

23

(racehorses all have to have different names and they are running out of normal horse names, which is why some of them are getting really weird now, such as Who Shot the Barman). But Blue is no longer a racehorse. He's a pacer and kept breaking into a trot or canter on the track, so I got him instead. Unfortunately he now seems to want to redeem himself, because with me he sometimes breaks out of a trot or a canter and into pacing, and it's really weird to sit on a horse when it's pacing along the sand on the beach.

I jump over the fence and check his cover. Blue has a love–hate relationship with his cover (he's a complicated horse). If I put it on he gets rub marks and if I leave it off he gets mud sores from the rain and from rolling in his paddock. I try to do fifty-fifty when it's wet like this. He's a fifteen-point-two hands chestnut (even though he's called Blue) gelding. Boy horses are either stallions or geldings. Geldings have had their bits removed so they're easier to handle. It makes them calmer. Not that he's had everything removed. He likes to let it all hang out. It's so good people wear clothes.

Blue turns his head, his mouth full of hay, to watch me as I walk around his back, dragging his cover so it's straight, tugging a piece of gorse out of his tail. He came from the racing stable down the road, next to the cemetery. His former owner died a couple of years ago from a stroke and Mum and Dad went to the funeral (I had to go to school that day). His son now runs the place. Mum said they had all the horses from the stable in the paddock next to the graves and they had all stood quietly, their heads bowed over the fence when the last words were said by the minister, as if they were praying just like all the people standing around the grave. And then, when they lowered the coffin, all the horses suddenly whinnied loudly, reared up and galloped away. Mum told me this with tears in her eyes.

I give Blue a hug around his neck and he nudges me back with his head, still chewing hay. When the rain stops we'll go for a ride. Not that the rain is the problem, it's more about damaging the paddock and every grass verge we ride on. The rain makes the ground soft and Blue isn't that light and he'll leave hoofprints everywhere and damaged paddocks don't grow grass and grass is better than hay for him to eat. Sorry, Blue. Maybe we can go out on the beach one day soon.

I climb over the fence again and push back the wet hair plastered to my forehead. Blue suddenly stamps one of his feet, and kicks out at his cover, snorting loudly.

'What's got into you?' I ask.

He pushes against me with his head, his mouth still full of hay. Some of it drops to the ground on my side of the fence.

I sigh and pick it up, stuff it back into his mouth for him, being careful of his teeth.

'There, settle down.'

But his ears are back. He's not listening to me. Maybe he's finally smelt the smoke from the explosion and the fire. Something has spooked him.

I give him a final rub on the neck, promise him a carrot later on, if I can steal one from the fridge without Mum catching me, and turn away. I haven't shut the feed shed door. The shed is about the same age as our house, circa Iron Age, or maybe early Roman, and if I don't shut the door the rain will get inside and make the hay damp. Blue gives me another snort as I pull the door shut. Complicated horse.

'See you later,' I tell him and walk back to the house to see if Mum has calmed down yet.

She hasn't. Dad hasn't gone back to bed, either.

There are more reporters knocking on our door wanting to find out what we saw, what we know, did we take pictures?

Dad isn't laughing anymore. I can tell he's straining to be polite. He goes outside and talks to one of the police on the road. I watch from my bedroom through a gap between the tarpaulin and the window frame. There's a lot of nodding and pointing, and then Dad comes back inside with a look of satisfaction on his face and a cop in uniform spends the rest of the afternoon guarding our front gate.

4

That evening we get a phone call from the police. They've finally decided it's most unlikely that Pete was in his house when it blew up, although they don't tell us how they've figured that out. Maybe they had a forensic team in, like on *CSI*, looking for DNA amid the wreckage of what's left. Or maybe it would have been obvious and any cop, or even me, could figure it out just by looking. A body blown up then burnt would still leave behind bones – maybe shattered burnt bones, but still bones, surely. Or maybe there would have just been an outline of where he was standing when it all happened. Or where he was lying, if he was *sleeping it off*. Maybe they expected to find his blackened skull still on his pillow in his bedroom. But they didn't, so that's why they think he escaped somehow. Except that wouldn't be right, because the pillow would have got burnt too, and the sheets and the mattress and the bed, along with his bedroom and everything else.

Maybe the cops knew all along that Pete wasn't in there but just didn't want to admit that somehow he had given them the slip when his house was surrounded by the Armed Offenders Squad, which is, remember, supposed to be the country's elite armed police force.

Anyway, they want all the neighbours to keep a lookout and to ring them straightaway if they see anything unusual, whatever that means.

'Do they think he'll be hiding somewhere, in some-one's garage?' Mum asks when Dad hangs up the phone.

'He'll be long gone.'

'We've only got the carport and there's nowhere in there for anyone to hide,' Mum says. 'And the horse shed, I suppose.'

'You fed Blue today?' Dad asks me.

'There was no one in there.'

'You sure?'

'I think I would have noticed, Dad.'

'Should we go check it now, just in case?' Mum asks.

'I'm not going out in the dark and the rain,' Dad says. 'And what if I did find him? You'd probably want me to invite him in for something to eat. Shall we make up the spare bed now?'

'There was no one in there.'

'I'll go check the shed.' Mum gets up.

'Leave it. He'll be long gone,' Dad says.

'He wasn't in there.'

'Don't you have homework to do?' Dad says.

We're all in the living room watching reruns of *Top Gear* on TV. Unlike Pete we don't have Sky TV, or used to have Sky TV.

'That would mean I had gone to school today and had homework given to me.'

Dad gives me a don't-be-so-smart look as Mum sits back down next to him on the sofa, then turns his attention again to Jeremy Clarkson trying to make a caravan fly. In only another couple of hours he should go to work, and with the sirens and the reporters and the police this afternoon and then the glazier coming to fix the windows he didn't get back to sleep after being woken by the explosion. He hates shift work, we hate him doing shift work, but he still does it. Got to eat, he says.

Dad drives the coal trains from the bins at Ngakawau below the open-cast Stockton Mine to Otira at Arthur's Pass. There a Canterbury driver swaps with him and takes the train through to Lyttelton Port near Christchurch where the coal is loaded onto ships to be delivered to India or China or South Africa. Stockton coal is not dirty coal, it's the best in the world. Our coal is hard and shiny and it burns too hot to use on the fire. And we don't use it to make electricity like they do in Australia and in Europe, pumping smoke into the atmosphere, causing greenhouse gasses and global warming. Our coal is used to make steel. Steel is iron with carbon added, and that carbon comes from our coal. Even the greenies need steel, because that's what bicycles are made out of. Not that most of them cycle anywhere anyway: they still use cars just like the rest of us.

The coal goes by rail to Lyttelton because we don't have a port big enough here on the coast for the ships that carry it – the Westport river port is too small, too shallow. There's been talk, lots of talk, about building a jetty out into the bay near the mine but no one has enough money to do it, and anyway, the rail tracks are already there and the trains and the train drivers and Lyttelton Port with its coal-handling facilities.

I do think Dad likes driving the coal trains, even though he doesn't like the hours. He sits in the front one of the two engines and behind him are thirty wagons, each with fifty tonnes of coal in them. That's one thousand, five hundred tonnes (a normal car weighs about two tonnes) plus the weight of the wagons and the two diesel engines heading south down the coast, then inland following the Buller River steadily climbing to the Southern Alps. He says out of his office window he sees some of the best scenery in the world, when he's not driving through the dark. Why would he want to do anything else? There's the coast with its sheer mountains on one side and farmland squeezed between them and sea, and then into the Buller River Gorge where the tracks hug the sides of the rock walls and water drips from every tree and every overhang. After the many bridges in the gorge it's through to the Junction and then following the Inangahua River through farmland until Reefton, where he leaves the river and passes through Maimai and Mawheraiti and Ikamatua and Ahaura until Stillwater. There the coal train does a left turn and instead of heading into Greymouth rumbles along the Arnold Valley to Lake Brunner and Jacksons and finally to Otira deep in the Southern Alps. From raging seas to snow-capped mountains, Dad says he sees it all, travels through it all and then back again in one shift. He says dawn, wherever it finds him, is always breathtaking.

At Otira, the Canterbury driver takes the train through the almost ten-kilometre long Otira Rail Tunnel built into the rock a hundred years ago. It's pretty cool. Because of the length of the tunnel they used to have electric trains, because steam trains would get choked up with all the smoke. The tunnel had its own coal-fired power station to make electricity for the tunnel. Now they use extractor fans so the diesels can get through and the driver carries oxygen, just in case. But Dad, he gets into the empty train that the driver has brought up from Lyttelton and brings it back to here to be loaded again.

A million tonnes of Stockton coal goes along that railway line every year. It used to be more, when the mine was doing okay. Maybe one day things will get better and they'll shift a million and a half or even two million again like they used to.

If they don't close the mines down altogether.

5

When I wake up the next morning, only one thing is going around in my head. I stare at my ceiling, the grey light coming through the curtains, and think. The shed door. I shut it twice yesterday when I fed Blue. I got the hay and shut it and then threw the hay over the fence and then I fixed his cover and then climbed back over the fence and had to shut the door again. And Blue was acting up. How could I have been so stupid? How did I not realise?

Dad is home from work and has started banging around the kitchen making himself breakfast. I've got the plate of sliced corned beef left over from last night out of the fridge on the bench. Mum has told me to make my school lunch with it. I don't like cold corned beef. It's gross. I make a heap of sandwiches with corned beef, mustard, lettuce, and I add a mandarin and an apple and a couple of muesli bars to the pile as well.

'You sure you've got enough sandwiches there?' Dad asks, looking at them.

'Just lunch,' I say, stuffing the whole lot into my lunchbox.

Mum's calling me from the hallway to hurry up and get in the car.

'I just want to check on Blue. Won't take a second,' I tell her as we leave by the back door, goodbyes to Dad said. I run out of the carport, my schoolbag over my shoulder and head to the shed. Blue whinnies at me.

'It's okay,' I tell him, slipping my lunchbox out of my schoolbag. I open the feed shed door but only a crack, just enough so I can shove the lunchbox in through the gap, and push it along the concrete floor as far as I can without looking. Then I slam the door shut and run back to Mum. She already has the car backed out of the carport.

'How was Blue?' Mum asks as I climb into the car.

'He's all right. Even after everything yesterday.'

'He's a horse. He'll be fine.'

Mum pulls out of the driveway, looking both ways and then motors it onto the road. On my side the police tape hangs limp in the drizzle around the blackened wreck of what remains of Pete's house. I wonder how long it will stay like that. Will someone buy the land, build a new house? Will we have new neighbours? But maybe no one can buy it, because Pete can't be found to sell it. And anyway, property isn't selling much in Westport because of the mines. The whole town is for sale, but no one is buying.

◆ ◆ ◆

School is the usual. A few kids ask me about the explosion, a few of the teachers too. I shrug it off as no big deal. I catch up on what I missed yesterday. Buy a filled roll from the canteen for lunch. Check what's going on in the world on my phone. Hear from everyone how badly we lost the school interchange. As if I really need to know. As if I really want to know.

I do have friends, but high school is not the same as primary school. My best friends are now at boarding school either in Nelson or Christchurch. It's partly because they're Catholic and there is no Catholic high school in Westport, but really it's because their parents think big schools in big cities are better than a small country high school in a coal town where it rains a lot. They're probably right. Dad says the only ones left at the high school besides me are the crims, the dopeheads and the girls who are three months pregnant. But that's just Dad being Dad. It's not really like that. It's just his joke.

Mum and Dad gave me the option of going to boarding school – they could afford it, just – but I didn't want to leave and they didn't want me to leave either. Home is home, even though my primary school friends are now gone for most of the year. It's just the way it is.

Mum picks me up after school, takes me home and I change out of my school uniform.

'I'm going to see Blue,' I call out to Mum. I grab my riding coat from the carport and head out to him. Blue is at the back of his paddock, but as soon as he sees me he races the length of it, his cover flapping, mud flying.

'So, Blue, how's things?' I ask him, rubbing his head over the fence. The feed shed door is shut behind me.

He snorts.

He's a happy horse today, no ears back, no eyes wild like yesterday. He stands and shudders, water flying everywhere, and swishes his tail. He just wants his hay and maybe to go for a ride. *Can we go for a ride, please, Annie, can we go for a ride?* he's asking me.

I turn my back on him and face the shed door, cautiously push it open, listen, look in. No one is in there. But my school lunchbox is empty, sitting on Blue's bale of hay. The mandarin peel is on the top. I do a double take. It's been shaped into letters – *TY*.

My heart is beating so fast it takes me another minute before I get it. *Thank you.* He's saying thank you for the sandwiches. So I was right. Pete was hiding here yesterday afternoon, last night, this morning.

But where has he gone?

I grab a rope from the shed, open the gate and run over to Blue, clip the rope to the halter's metal circle under his chin and lead him out of the paddock to the tree by the fence. He lets me, his ears up. He knows what it means. I quickly tie the rope to the tree branch as always and start unbuckling his cover. He stamps one foot as I haul the cover off and throw it on the fence, then rush back into the shed for his saddle blanket, saddle and bridle. The saddle is a Wintec, so it's reasonably light. I should brush him first but there's no time, so it's saddle blanket on, then the Wintec. I knee him in the guts and quickly do up the girth strap tight, my head holding up the saddle flap, before he can puff out his stomach again, then yank down the stirrups on their straps.

I give him a hasty rub between the eyes before slipping on his bridle, the bit flat in my palm until he accepts it between his teeth. I unclip the halter rope, lead Blue away from the tree and jump on. I did pony club for a year (at Mum and Dad's insistence) but gave it up as soon as I could. Pony club would not have approved of my mounting style this afternoon.

Blue starts walking as soon as I'm on and I pull him around so we're heading for the gap in the scrub at the back of our property. It leads to the beach. I've given up on the hood of my raincoat and my hair is now slick from the drizzle, but it doesn't matter – I've caught sight of what I've been looking for.

It's a footprint in the mud, and it shouldn't be there. I lean over Blue's side searching for more. He flicks his tail but doesn't complain further about his unbalanced load. Most of this track is hard, but there is the odd patch of mud – and sure enough, there is another footprint, a boot print. They're heading towards the beach. I steer Blue carefully, making sure his hoofprints are covering them, backing him up where I need to.

The scrub is mostly manuka and fern, some gorse, and matted long grass on the side of the sandy track. Then there's a steep slope that Blue plunges down without a pause, with me leaning back, and we're onto the beach where Deadmans Creek meets the surf. The footprints are easier to follow now in the deep sand.

We wade through Deadmans, me hitching my feet up against the saddle so I don't get wet, and find the footprints again on the other side. It means Pete must have made it through at low tide, mid-morning, or it would have been too deep for him to get across. We take even greater care now concealing his footprints, Blue obligingly scuffing his hooves in the rain-soaked sand and doing the job perfectly. I look back, one hand on his rump, checking.

Blue whinnies and I turn around. Another horse is on the beach. It's jet black, and it's galloping full tilt at an old tree that's been washed up on the beach from a flood. The tree is standing almost upright, its huge root ball sitting on the sand, a broken trunk above it. The branches are long gone. Blue stops and watches, and I let him. The rider has the reins loose, using his body to urge the horse on. When they get to the tree the horse skirts around it like it's done it a million times before, almost turning on the spot before galloping back to where it started, sand flying under its hooves. There they stop, the rider rubbing the horse's neck and collecting the reins, his horse's sides heaving under the western saddle.

Blue whinnies again (thanks for that, Blue) and they both look our way. Blue starts walking towards them and I push him into a trot, rising perfectly as pony club taught me. I'm still following the footprints in the sand, scuffing them out, but I can see they stop where the black horse has been working. Pete must have walked past the driftwood tree this morning.

'An old racehorse,' the rider says when we get close enough.

I stop Blue and push his wet mane over to hide his racing brand, white against his chestnut-brown neck, before I think about what I'm doing.

'He's not old,' I reply.

'He looks nice. Is he fast?'

'He can be.'

'Want to race?'

I look at him. Blue shifts under me, his ears forward, as if he knows exactly what the rider has suggested. The boy is older than me, maybe by a year, two. His riding jacket is done up tightly around him; he has black riding pants and boots. He's not wearing a helmet, but nor am I. I usually do but I forgot it today. The rain has darkened his hair. His face is tanned, so he's not from here. No one gets a suntan in this weather. And he's smiling at me, or it's really more of a grin. White teeth. And then he turns his horse, facing it away down the Fairdown Beach, and suddenly they're off.

Blue moves beneath me, a cautious step, then another, waiting for my decision. I sigh, shake my head and give him the smallest nudge with my feet, and he lurches forward with both front legs into a full gallop. I stand up, out of the saddle, shortening the reins, my hands hard up either side of his neck, my face not far above them, raincoat flying. I should have done the zip up.

6

Although Blue was a pacer, I've always thought he should have been a galloper. He's a thoroughbred in disguise. With his longer stride we soon catch the black horse, which is probably already exhausted from racing around the tree, and the boy looks at me sideways, curious, then urges his black horse on. We're neck and neck, side by side, maybe a metre apart, galloping down the beach on the hard sand just in front of the waves. If anyone describes galloping to you as the same as flying, don't let them fool you. Okay, I've never flown, of course, not like a bird, but I imagine it's not like this. For starters you're connected to this animal that seems like nothing but fluid, moving muscle beneath you. And you're connected by only a small section of the soles of your riding boots balancing on the stirrups, the insides of your legs clamped against the moving sides of the horse and your hands gripping the reins. Nothing else. Yet you move as one – horse and rider. Forward. Fast. So fast you can hardly breathe in the air as it rushes past you, so fast the sand beneath you is a blur. And I'm crouching, but it feels as if I'm balancing on a tightrope. One move from me could send us both crashing down. The same with Blue – a sidestep, a stumble on some soft sand, and I'd be off, cartwheeling down the beach. Galloping is trust and honesty between horse and rider and pure, amazing energy.

I could stand up, let go of the reins, put my arms out like wings, my raincoat already flapping behind me, and then maybe it would be like flying. I've seen people do that, on YouTube, stand on their horses bareback, do hand-stands, tricks. But I've never tried it. Not yet.

Out of the corner of my eye I can see the boy watching me, but I keep looking between Blue's ears, looking for any-thing on the sand that might trip us up, that Blue or the other horse might startle at. But there's nothing and we keep going, just endless beach in front of us, waves to our left, grey late-afternoon sky somewhere above and the horizon muddled in the misty rain. It's a day made for galloping.

I can feel Blue ease into his stride. He's content now to match the other horse. His competitiveness, the desire to win bred into him, is being dampened by his curiosity. And he's probably getting tired. He's not used to this. He hasn't been out of his paddock for days, plus we don't regularly gallop down the beach. I'm not a thrillseeker and neither is Blue. If anything, he's a bit of a wimp.

I let my grip on the reins loosen, relax my shoulders. Enjoy it. Blue is managing to keep pace with the black horse, even though it is fitter-looking. It's not a race anymore, just two horses and their riders going for a gallop in the misty rain. Up ahead, somewhere, is the mouth of the Whareatea River, going out to sea. It's too deep for the horses to gallop through, even to swim across, when it's been raining like this. We will have to stop there, but until then it's just beach and the rhythm of the horses' hooves on the sand.

But the other horse is suddenly on a collision course with us, the boy's legs banging hard into mine, his hand reaching out and grabbing at Blue's reins. Blue almost rears up but I react quickly enough to push him down, my weight forward and down into the saddle. My head snaps back, whiplashed by the abrupt stop.

'What did you do that for?' I yell at the boy, trying to calm Blue, trying to calm myself, trying to stay on and not fall off, the two horses still jostling each other in the drizzle.

'Look,' he says, and I do what he says and hear it for the first time over the surf: a helicopter, low, heading straight towards us down the beach.

'It would have made the horses bolt. Sorry, I just wanted to slow you down. I didn't think your horse would react that way.'

I watch the helicopter, half listening to him, still trying to settle Blue. It's a big helicopter, not as big as the logging ones, but bigger than a two-seater. It's like the one that was flying over our house after the explosion yesterday. I have the reins back now but Blue is far from still. It's the same with the other horse. They're both jumpy with a helicopter so close. But there's only one thought in my mind. What I came to the beach for. What I should have been doing instead of galloping with this boy.

I whirl Blue around and head back the way we came.

'Hey, where are you going?' the boy calls out but I ignore him, already in a canter. I'm sitting down in the saddle, safe, just in case the helicopter does startle Blue. I don't want to come off. The helicopter is behind us, moving slowly, and maybe that's all it's going to do, if it doesn't leave altogether. The uprooted driftwood tree is still a way off.

Blue stretches into the canter and it's just the two of us. I don't look back to see what has happened to the boy and his horse. Or to see the helicopter.

I'm looking for more footsteps in the sand, but so far there are only the horses' tracks from when we galloped the other way. Hopefully it will stay that way. Hopefully

Pete is long gone and not sitting somewhere in the scrub at the edge of the beach, or snoozing next to a piece of driftwood in plain sight from the air.

The drizzle is turning into rain, pitting the sand, the horses' hoofprints, the tide mark, but I keep searching, angry with myself for forgetting what I came here for. The noise from the helicopter is steadily getting louder. And then it's suddenly on top of us, the downwash from its rotors filling the air with water. Blue's ears are flattened in fear. I pull him up and slide off him quickly, hauling his nose, as much of his head as I can, into my open raincoat. He wants to run, to get away from the noise, but I hold him tight and he stands there, shuddering, his head pressed hard against my chest. I glare upwards, water in my eyes, but no one is there to see me, no one hanging out the helicopter doors looking down.

'It's okay it's okay it's okay it's okay,' I say into Blue's ears. And we just stay there, Blue cowering in my arms. Then at last the helicopter moves away, flies off over the sea, cutting the corner of the bay to Westport. I don't know. I don't care. It's gone. Blue's shudders slowly subside. He's wet, cold; we both are. I need to get him home, get him dry, the sweat off him, before he gets crook. Get some feed into him. Do something. I jump back on and we start for home. Blue sets the pace – a fast walk is all he can manage. We skirt the driftwood tree. There are no footprints to be seen on this side of it, just the other horse's hoofprints from where it was circling, the whole area of sand churned up. Pete must have walked to the tree, then up into the scrub. Lucky. Lucky that the boy and his horse covered his tracks. I stand up in the stirrups and scan the land above the beach as best I can, but there's nothing. And I'm not going looking, not with Blue like this.

We plod towards Deadmans, Blue going slower and slower with every step. I'm going to have to get off and lead him. There's a noise behind us: the other horse and its rider. I glance back before I can stop myself.

'What happened?' he asks, when our horses are side by side. Blue picks up the pace, snorting.

'Stupid helicopter.'

'What was it doing? It was right over you.'

I don't answer.

'Is your horse okay?'

'He'll be fine. I just want to get him home.' Which I realise too late is the worst thing to say. We're at Deadmans. The boy and his horse stop on the bank and watch as Blue and I wade through the water. I don't turn around, but I know he's watching as we go the short distance further along the beach and then up the bank. I don't know anything about him but now he knows where I live.

7

Mum is pulling wallpaper off the hallway wall. I'm inside getting some hot water to mix with molasses for Blue. I want to ask her what she's doing, but Blue is my first priority. He needs something warm after what he's been through. I've already washed and rubbed him down to get the sweat off him before I put his cover on, and when I get back with the bucket of water he knows exactly what's next and whinnies his thanks. I mix in the molasses and oats and rub his neck as he eats, his head deep in the bucket.

Back inside I grab a towel from the bathroom to dry my hair, then stand there, watching Mum. She's started at my bedroom door and there's about a square metre of missing wallpaper. It's coming off in tiny bits. I've never liked the hallway wallpaper. It's tiny pink flowers with green leaves on a white background, and you can't tell if the flowers are upside down or they're supposed to be like that. Whoever owned the house before us must have put it up.

'What are you doing?' I finally ask.

'Stripping wallpaper. I want to paint the hallway. Make it nicer.'

She has the light on. The hallway is always dark when it's raining outside. Apart from the front door with its lead-light coloured glass surround, the only other light filters from the doorways of the rooms that lead off it.

'What colour are you going to paint it?'

'I don't know. Something pale, I suppose.' She sits back on her heels and looks at me. 'Nice ride? Where did you go?'

'Just down the beach. The paddock is too boggy.'

'Blue okay after the explosion yesterday?'

'I think so.'

'You worry about that horse too much. Here, give me a hand.'

I crouch down beside her. Even with the light on it's still gloomy. She's using a small knife from the kitchen, one she usually cuts up vegetables with, trying to slide it under the edge of the wallpaper and then rip it from the wall.

'There's more wallpaper underneath,' I say.

'I know. I reckon there are about five layers.'

'So people have just wallpapered over the wallpaper?'

'Looks like it.'

'What, for a hundred years? Isn't that how old the house is?'

'I think so.'

'So why don't we just paint over the wallpaper?'

'Because I want it to look nice.'

I slide a finger under a loose piece of wallpaper and tug and it tears off in a depressingly small jagged piece.

'This is going to take forever.'

'Just give me ten minutes of your time.'

Underneath the upside-down pink flowers are wide brown and gold stripes. Who would have put that up? And then there's a blue and teal pattern. Slightly nicer.

'Did they have wallpaper a hundred years ago?'

'I think they used to import it from England. It wouldn't have been like wallpaper today. Some of it was handpainted. But it was still wallpaper.'

Mum hands me her knife and I use it to get under an edge of the teal and pull like crazy. All three layers come off in one reasonably large piece.

'Well done,' Mum says and gets up, walks down the hallway. She comes back with another knife from the kitchen for her to use.

When Dad comes in an hour later, we're still in the hallway pulling wallpaper off the wall together.

'What a mess,' Dad says.

'Got to make a mess sometimes,' Mum says, brushing the pieces from her jeans.

He pulls a patch slowly off the wall, trying to make it as large as possible before it tears but failing badly. 'Big job.'

'Well, we've made a start. I must admit it's oddly addictive. Like doing a jigsaw puzzle. How was the meeting?'

'Not good,' he says and leaves it at that.

'I'll dish up tea,' Mum says and follows him into the kitchen. 'Five minutes, Annie?'

'Okay.'

Which in other words means *I want to talk to Dad alone for five minutes in the kitchen about stuff you're not meant to know about.* Do they think I'm dumb? It will be about Dad's work. Some meeting about what will happen with the railway if the coalmines close. It's just not the miners who will be affected, but everyone. The mechanics that look after the diggers and the trucks, the people who look after the roads up to the mine, the train drivers who take the coal to Lyttelton. And then when people start leaving to find work elsewhere it will be the supermarkets and the pubs and all the shops and the schools. They're saying in the newspaper the town could halve in size overnight if the mines close. Become a ghost town.

I pull a piece of teal paper from the wall. Under it is another layer of pink flowers. Roses this time, big petals. I wonder if it they were handpainted and who by, when? Even if they weren't, someone must have done the original design. Laboured over each leaf, painting each thorn on the stems, the water droplets at the edge of the bottom petal. Someone far away.

'Annie, tea,' Mum calls from the kitchen.

We eat casserole from plates on our laps, watching the news on TV. Syria, Iraq, Turkey, the US, Europe. The news presenters 'caution' us about the 'disturbing images' they're 'about to show'.

'Then why show them?' Dad says, his forkful of food poised halfway to his mouth.

Mum and I don't say anything and all three of us watch the bombed hospitals, the dying kids, the men with guns.

Afterwards I have homework to do, even though it's Friday night. It's better getting it out of the way than having it hanging over my head all weekend. I don't hear Dad leaving for work. The wind has come up and above the rain on the roof there is the roar of the surf on the beach in the distance. I fall asleep listening to the waves.

◆ ◆ ◆

The next morning when I go to get breakfast, Mum and Dad are talking again, waiting for the toaster to pop.

'Wouldn't be the ideal way to get rid of a body,' Mum's saying. 'Could end up anywhere on that beach, especially with that storm last night. Those currents are fierce.'

'Could have got eaten by the sharks,' Dad says, getting the marmalade out of the cupboard. 'Nothing to find then. Lots of sharks out there.'

'Just be careful if you go riding on the beach,' Mum says, waving a butter knife at me.

'Why?'

'I heard they're searching the beaches with helicopters, looking for a body.'

'Pete's? Do they think he's dead?'

'No, someone else. Someone Pete was mixed up with.'

'They think Pete murdered someone? Is that why the police surrounded his house?'

'They surrounded his house because he shot up the police station the night before because he got drunk and was dumb. Please, just stay off the beach.'

I haven't got time to take Blue out anyway, on the beach or anywhere. It's Saturday morning and I've got basketball practice. And since we didn't win the game against Kaiapoi High School, our coach will be working us hard.

I bike past the remains of Pete's house, still guarded by the police tape, past the cemetery, over the Orowaiti Bridge and along Brougham Street. There's no traffic, there's never any traffic; it's just that it's raining. It's been raining for a whole week now.

At the courts there are drills and more drills. Liam, our coach, used to work up the hill in the coalmines, seven days on, seven days off, so we only saw him one week out of two, but now he's always here. He lost his job a couple of weeks back. There's no other work in town, but he can't sell his house. So he's stuck in Westport, coaching basketball, for which he doesn't get paid, but should, because he's a good coach. He got paid for digging up coal, which now the world doesn't want, but he doesn't get paid for coaching basketball to kids who want him, who need him. And we do need him. In this town there's nothing else for us to do but play sport – netball, rugby, hockey, basketball, athletics. I'm just glad I figured out early on it's a good idea to pick a sport that's played inside.

The sound of basketballs hitting the wooden floor echoes the rain pounding on the gym roof. Samantha's shoes squelch every time she moves. She must have worn them here. Sam is in most of my classes. We hang around together a bit. Really, she should have come with dry shoes. There are little puddles of water now all over the courts where we have dripped, and Liam runs around with a towel trying to mop them up before we slip over. Not that we ever do. We're used to it. The air is humid from the dampness, and after ten minutes of drills the sweat is pouring off us all. Even Liam, who is bald with a round face that gets redder and redder as practice goes on. We don't make fun of him. For starters his own kids are here bouncing balls as they watch from the sidelines, still too young to play; plus he knows our parents; and also we just don't do that type of thing.

After twenty minutes of drills he stops us and talks about the rest of the season, how we have to put the one bad game behind us, and how he wants us all to have individual goals as well as team goals. Then he divides us into two teams and we start to play.

'Hey, Annie,' he says, stopping me. 'We really needed you the other day.'

'I know. I just couldn't make it.'

'I think you had a good excuse. We'll play them again next year.'

After our allotted hour is finished, he calls it quits and sends us all home, back out into it. After the sweatbox the gym has become, it's good to be in the fresh air. I pedal as fast as I can down Brougham Street wondering, for the countless time, if less or more rain falls on you the faster you go. Or is it the time spent out in the rain that matters, instead of whether you're standing still or moving? It's a question for the TV show *MythBusters*, if they haven't answered it already.

8

Whoever designed our house must have had a sense of humour. It's a rectangle, with the shorter sides the front and the back of the house. At the back is a carport – a covered area where we park the car and leave our coats and gumboots by the door and where Dad hangs up the overalls he wears for work. At the front is a wooden veranda. There are three steps dead-centre from the path that lead to the porch and front door. Above the veranda is a curved corrugated iron roof, and then there is the triangular shape of the real roof. On either side of the front door are big sash windows (the windows to my bedroom and my parent's bedroom) that have folded-down blinds on the inside. Mum made them, so maybe she was in on the joke as well.

If you look at the house from the front, it's like a face – the two windows are the eyes, the blinds Mum made are the eyelids, the door is the nose, the porch is the mouth, the steps up to it is the tongue and the veranda roof is the eyebrows. Last year I borrowed Mum's good camera, on a day it wasn't raining, put it in the front garden on a tripod, which I'd borrowed from school, and made a film clip for YouTube of the house winking and then closing its eyes by letting the blinds up and down and taking photographs. It was pretty cool. Last time I checked it had over fifty thousand views. So I'm partly famous; well, the false name I used for the clip is.

Even though the house isn't smiling, it's not frowning or angry or sad. I think it's a happy face, a serene face, an I-can-cope-with-anything face. It's the face I wear every time I head through that front door, coming or going. And it makes me feel like I belong here. It gives me strength. This house has been here for so long, has survived the rain and the storms, so if it can, then so can I. I am a West Coaster, and this is my home, my place of belonging. It is who I am. Even though it rains here a lot.

I'm not sure if Blue feels the same way, or knows any different. He's lived his whole life here on the same road (apart from going to races), and he's older than me too. None of which he probably thinks about, especially as we splash across Deadmans, its surface pockmarked by the raindrops. He has his ears forward. Maybe he's watching for helicopters or maybe he's on the lookout for the black horse from yesterday. Forget that, Blue. They won't be here again. Twice in two days would be too much of a coincidence. I know what I'm looking for and that's a body. If Pete did murder someone, I want to know, and Mum said at breakfast this morning this is where the police are searching. High tide was a couple of hours ago. Let's see if anything has washed up.

I nudge Blue into a slow canter just below the tide mark and keep my eyes on the line of driftwood and seaweed. I've never seen anything particularly interesting on this beach apart from a dead seal. My parents know of someone who once found a dead penguin. He put it in his freezer and would bring it out at parties as a kind of joke. The last I heard of it was it went skiing on a Canterbury ski field. They took photos of it and put them on Facebook. You couldn't have done that with the seal I found. It was too far gone. It stank real bad. Even my horse didn't like the smell.

Blue has suddenly picked up the pace and is whinnying. I take my eyes off the line of driftwood and look ahead to see the black horse, riding around the same dead tree washed up on the beach. It could be yesterday all over again.

I slow Blue to a walk, just in case he thinks we're going to take off down the beach at a gallop like last time, and the boy sees us and pulls his horse to a stop. The horse paws the ground. Maybe it doesn't want to meet us, but it's obvious the boy does.

'I thought I would have to come here every afternoon for days until you came back,' he says, his head tilted to one side.

'Why?' I ask.

'To see you again, of course. I didn't even find out your name yesterday.'

'I didn't find out yours either.'

'It's Jack. Jack Robertson. This is Tassie. She's a rodeo horse, for barrel racing. You know, when you go round a barrel?'

'I know what it is.'

'I go to rodeos all around the country and in Australia, the States and Canada. Although Tassie doesn't go over there, not to North America. It's too expensive.'

'We don't have a rodeo in Westport. Not a real one.'

'I'm not here for a rodeo.'

I'm not going to ask the obvious question. Actually, I have lots of questions, especially as I'm pretty sure guys don't do barrel racing. It's a girls-only sport. And was that what he was doing riding around that dead tree? But I sit and wait to see what he'll say. His horse – Tassie – is picking up her feet, like she wants to go. She doesn't want to stand here and talk in the rain. Blue is perfectly still, just his ears moving, listening. I've got the reins in one hand, waiting.

'My dad is here for work. So I came too – never been here before – and we brought Tassie over, because she needs to be exercised. Because of the circuit, the rodeo circuit, I do school by correspondence, so I can pretty well go wherever.'

Blue puts his ears forward. I bet he's thinking the same as I am. This boy does a lot of talking about himself.

'Tassie's a quarter horse,' he says and then he suddenly shuts up, like he's run out of things to say, or he's realised what Blue and I are thinking. 'I still don't know your name,' he finishes.

'What does your dad do?'

'He's a cop. Well, a detective. They think this drug dealer has been murdered but they can't find the body, and the guy they think did it blew up his house the other day so they're pretty worried because he might blow up something else. That's why we're here.'

I put my empty hand on my knee and lean forward, stretch out my back in the saddle. Absolutely brilliant. So when I was using Blue to scuff out Pete's footprints on the beach yesterday I was destroying police evidence right in front of the detective's teenage son. I wonder if I can be charged with that.

'Was it him in the helicopter yesterday?' I ask.

'No. I told him, though. It was some other cops. He was going to talk to them. That was pretty dangerous, what they did. You got home all right? Your horse is okay?'

'Blue's fine.'

'Blue. That's a nice name, for a chestnut.'

'What were they doing in the helicopter?'

'I don't know. Dad doesn't talk much about work. He's kind of the silent type.'

I don't reply, but I have to try really hard not to laugh.

'Do you, I don't know, want to ride down the beach? You were heading that way anyway,' Jack asks. He looks over at me nervously, obviously worried that I won't say yes.

'Okay.'

'Not galloping this time.'

'Okay.'

I use my legs to push Blue forward and he starts off at a walk. The black falls in beside us, shaking her wet mane. I have more time to look at her today. She's fit, I can see that, and compact. She's got a small head but a huge chest, all muscle. I'm trying to remember everything I know about quarter horses, which is about zero. Cowboys ride them. They come from ranches in America, where they're used for stock work and for competing in barrel racing.

'Do you do roping?' I ask.

'I'm starting to learn, but I'm useless so far. It's not as easy as it looks.'

'Bull riding?'

'I'm not that crazy.'

'So what do you do? You don't barrel race. That's what girls do.'

He glances at me sharply and then looks away, out to sea, obviously deciding what to tell me, maybe embarrassed he's been caught out.

'I ride saddle bronc, but I busted up my shoulder so I'm out for several months. I was meant to go to the States to compete.'

'And that's where Tassie's owner is, isn't she, barrel racing?' I finish for him. 'You were meant to go on the circuit with her but she went on her own. So you're keeping her horse fit for her, for when she comes back.'

He nods. 'Her name is Stella. Tassie's her horse.'

Girlfriend or sister, I want to ask, *or just someone you know*? but I keep my mouth shut. My bets are on girlfriend. A girlfriend with a horse like Tassie and I'm on a retired racing hack. Just great.

So with me keeping my mouth shut and Jack finally keeping his shut as well, we walk along the beach. I'm still keeping my eye on the high tide line. I haven't forgotten why I'm out here this time.

'It rains a lot in Westport,' he says after a couple of minutes.

'It's just the wet season right now.'

'When is that?'

'It starts about the first of August and goes through until about the end of July.'

'Okay,' he says.

I look over at him and he's grinning. He's got the joke. Truce.

'My name is Annie.'

'Annie,' he repeats, smiling even more now. 'So you go to school here?'

'Buller High. It's the only high school here.'

'I'm guessing you're fifteen, sixteen?'

'Fifteen. I'll be sixteen in a couple of months, though. I live across the road from that house that got blown up.'

'Okay.'

'Watched it happen. They had the roads blocked off, so I couldn't get to school.'

'That must have been pretty awesome.'

'Woke my dad up. He does shift work, driving the coal trains.' Which is probably not as exciting as being a detective of murder investigations around the country.

'So you ride along this beach often?'

'Sometimes. It's a good place to ride when it's so wet. Doesn't mess up the grass.'

'And also you're looking for something.'

'Am I?'

'That's why you rode off the other day when the helicopter arrived, and that's what you're doing now.'

'Maybe.'

'It's kind of obvious. You know, seeing a dead body isn't that nice.'

'Have you seen one to know?'

'Just my mum's.'

I don't know how to answer.

'Sorry, I shouldn't have said that,' he mumbles.

'It's okay. I shouldn't have asked.'

'She died last year, cancer. So, you really think this dead body is washed up along here somewhere? Is that what you're doing?'

'Worth a look. This is where things end up usually. This beach or North Beach or the ones further north, that's the way the current takes them.'

'Won't be North Beach,' he says. 'They're not searching there. Someone saw the body dumped into the Orowaiti River. So it'll be this one.'

'I saw a raincoat floating down the Orowaiti. It was the day it started raining.'

9

Okay, I like Jack. I admit it. Blue likes Tassie. I'm not sure if Tassie likes Blue, but what does that matter? I like Jack not in *that* way, but in the 'I'm curious about him and I would like to have a go barrel racing Tassie' way. That's all. Except Jack competes in saddle bronc events in rodeos all around the world, and he looks like he competes in saddle bronc events in rodeos all around the world. Understand? Get the picture?

It's easy to imagine him wearing a cowboy hat.

So we ride for about an hour along the beach in the drizzle and we don't see any dead bodies, which I am kind of glad about because then I would have to explain to my parents what we were doing together when we found a body when really all we were doing was riding along the beach in the drizzle for about an hour talking about nothing, just talking, and at the end of it, when I turn to splash across Deadmans again and he goes off to where he's parked his four-wheel-drive and horse float (which means he must be old enough to have his driver's licence), we kiss, which on horseback isn't that easy, especially with Tassie refusing to stay still, so then we laugh. And we swap cell phone numbers. So maybe I do like him in that way. I'm not saying. He's got a girlfriend, remember.

I give Blue an extra ration of hay.

Mum has given up stripping wallpaper for the day. There's now a sizable chunk missing of the tiny pink flowers on the white background, and I think she might have even broken through the final layer to the wallboard. Although I'm not sure if it is wallboard. It looks dusty anyway, like bugs have been eating away at it. Gross. Actually I'm not sure where Mum is. I call out to her, but there's no reply. She could have gone for a run. She does that: gets cabin fever, as she puts it, because of the rain, and needs to blow off some steam. The rain affects people. Another week of it and the teachers will start to get grumpy at school. It always happens. Humans need sunshine. Popping vitamin D pills doesn't quite do it.

I find some dry clothes and put my wet ones in the ever-growing washing pile in the laundry. (Mum is obviously waiting for fine weather before she does any washing so she can hang clothes outside on the line rather than use the dryer – good luck with that one, Mum.) As I munch into a sandwich as a late lunch I open my laptop and go on Facebook, searching for Jack Robertson. He's easy to find – he's the Jack Robertson with spurs and a cowboy hat as his profile pic – but his page is obviously private. There's hardly anything on it. My finger hovers over the keyboard as I wonder if I should send a friend request, and I decide maybe not. Not yet, anyway. Instead I go on Google and type his name again. He's easy to find there too. Page after page about him competing at rodeos, winning at rodeos, breaking his collarbone at a big rodeo in Christchurch two months ago. There's even video footage of him going down, the horse catching him with its hind hooves. It's not easy to watch.

So at least he wasn't lying.

Just out of curiosity, I type my own name into Google. Nothing, nothing at all about me. Good. I like it like that.

I wonder if Jack is doing the same right now, but he's still probably rubbing Tassie down, feeding her. He said he and his father are staying out at the Cape, on the other side of Westport. He would have had to put her in the float, drive there, take her out, get her sorted. Maybe in another half hour he'll be opening his laptop, or turning on his tablet, or looking on his phone. So will he send me a friend request? But then, I didn't tell him my surname.

I watch the video again. Jack has on a black cowboy hat, black fringed chaps and a safety vest. He loses the hat with the horse's first buck, but he makes it to the buzzer at eight seconds. He's looking for the other rider, but he isn't close enough for him to grab and the horse bucks him again at a weird angle and he goes down, the horse's hooves making contact. Brutal.

But he doesn't stay down. It's obvious he's hurt, and hurt bad, but he gets to his feet somehow. The other rider temporarily blocks the camera's view as his horse and the horse Jack was on gallop past, and when they're gone, Jack is on his feet, walking towards where his hat is lying on the dirt. He's holding his injured arm with the other hand but he lets it go to reach down and pick up the hat, dust it off, put it back on his head. The announcer is asking everyone to cheer for him. And then the video ends.

Okay, he's the first boy who has kissed me. Not that it was a big deal. It was just fun. It was more bumping noses than anything because Tassie shifted her weight when Jack leaned out of the saddle and we didn't really connect. That's why we laughed. We both laughed. So it wasn't even a proper kiss. Even though the intention was there, at least from him it was. So first kiss, age fifteen (some girls around here are already pregnant at that age), and it was on horseback, with a guy who might have a girlfriend, who is currently on the other side of the world. What does all that say about me?

Mum comes home, supermarket bags in her hands (the other cure for cabin fever, according to her, is chocolate).

'Look who I found,' she calls out, and Samantha pops her head round my bedroom door.

'Okay if I come in?' Sam asks, and comes in anyway. She's been to my place before – usually courtesy of Mum, who thinks I need more friends – so she knows what's what. She flops herself down on my bed and stares at the ceiling. 'It's just dead boring at home.'

'It's dead boring here too,' I tell her.

'Come on, you have houses that blow up across the road and get you out of school for the day.'

'Besides that.'

'You still pissed off about the basketball game?' Sam has dark wavy hair and she does the bedraggled look perfectly. She's wearing the latest sports clothes, no doubt bought in Christchurch, because no shops here stock them.

'I should have been there.'

'Wasn't your fault. We were probably going to lose anyway, whether you were there or not.'

Thomas dispels the awkwardness perfectly by sauntering in at this point. He arches his back, demanding a rub, which I dutifully give him; then he sidles over to Sam to check out if she knows the Thomas-cat-etiquette protocol. Sam does, and adds a few extras, such as scratches behind the ears and tickles just above the nose. Not only can Sam suck up to my mother, she does the same with our cat.

'So, can we go look at it?' she asks.

'Look at what?'

'The blown-up house, of course.'

'That. Suppose so.'

'You mean you haven't already been over there?'

'Why would I?'

'Because.'

'We drive past it all the time. You can see it from the road.'

'Come on.'

'It's my neighbour's house.'

'It's not trespassing.'

I give up. At least now I know why she came round to see me. It wasn't just to harass me about basketball.

We grab our coats and go out the front door, avoiding Mum unpacking supermarket shopping in the kitchen. The road is empty when we cross it, the rain steady. Pete's driveway still has police tape strung over it. We straddle it and walk up the gravel.

'Not much left,' Sam says, stating the obvious. She's sucking a strand of wet hair.

I wander around to where the front door once was. It's kind of still there, just in large splintered, blackened pieces, most of it lying on the concrete steps. The steps seem to be the only part of the house that has survived undamaged. Sam has already climbed inside. She's standing there, looking around. There's no floor – it's gone, charred and blown up – so her feet are on the ground, between the concrete piles.

'It's hard to work out what was where,' she says.

'I think you're in what was the living room,' I tell her.

'How do you know?'

'Because at night you used to be able to see the TV through the window.'

She seems to accept my answer, because she doesn't reply. Minutes later she's holding up a large blackened piece of plastic. 'Part of the TV, do you reckon?'

'Could be. We probably shouldn't be touching stuff, just in case.'

'The police have finished, otherwise there would be a guard here or something. It's fine.'

I think about Jack's dad. Would he have stood where I'm standing? Searched through the remains? Or did he just read the reports? There were swarms of police here afterwards, on the Thursday afternoon and when I was at school yesterday, so I don't know what happened then. So maybe. Then again, maybe not.

'The guy who lived here, have they found him?'

'Don't know.'

Sam's rummaging through the wreckage at the back of the house, what looks like was once the kitchen. She holds up pots, a frying pan, broken plates. A fridge is lying on its side.

'Everything is just destroyed. There's nothing of any value at all,' she says.

'Is that why we're here? You hoping to pinch stuff?'

'No, although if there was, could sell them on Trade Me, I suppose.'

'Probably not a good idea.'

'I wasn't going to say where I got them from. No, I was just curious. You know how they talk about a blast pattern, how you can tell where the explosion was? But you can't tell anything here. It's just one big mess.'

I look around again, trying to work out if what she is saying is true. There's burnt wood, furniture, destroyed belongings everywhere. I can't figure out anything from it. It's just a charred, soaking-wet disaster zone. Coming over here, I'd half hoped I could have saved something for Pete, maybe a framed photo of his mum, some item of clothing, anything. But there is nothing to salvage. Sam's right. Everything is one big mess.

10

It's not what you expect to see when you're invited around by family friends for morning tea on a Sunday, on your dad's day off, even if you are told to bring gumboots. The Brown's farm is at the bottom of Mount Rochfort. My dad first met the Browns when his train bowled one of their cows. It was their fault – the cow shouldn't have been on the railway line but it had broken through one of the fences, and Dad couldn't have stopped, however much he tried. It takes a lot to stop a fully loaded coal train. The cow hadn't done any damage to the train, but the train had done a lot of damage to the cow. Dad didn't need to go and apologise to them afterwards, but he did, when his shift ended, and they have been friends ever since. Harry has taken Dad and me deer shooting up above the farm, and Mrs Brown, Di, is a great cook.

But when we get there it's not scones or biscuits. Not yet, anyway. Instead it's gumboots on, raincoats on, let's go for a walk. Mum and I share confused glances, but do as we're told. Dad likes getting out in the bush (it's a dairy farm, but there's a lot of bush too) so he strides ahead alongside Harry, with Di and Mum and me following. Di and Mum are chatting about the cows, the weather (when will it stop raining, if it will stop raining) and Di's grandchildren (she has seven, so she has a lot to talk about) as we walk along the muddy track. Harry has the gate open for us, waiting, and he does it back up after we walk through. In the paddock are the cows. They're golden Jerseys with big brown eyes and they stop eating the long grass as we walk by. Di reaches out and gives one a pat. The cows don't seem to mind the rain, but you can see where their hooves have sunk into the soft ground. Harry plants his gumboot on the single-wire fence on the edge of the paddock and we all step over it carefully. I know not to touch any of the fences here with my hands – they're electric and getting a shock from them is not much fun. They have to be electric, because that way the cows stay in their paddock with just one wire. The cows know not to touch it – they get a bigger shock with their four feet compared with our two. And it's just one wire because in a flood (it does flood here, I've seen it) it's easier to cut one wire to let the cows out so they don't drown than pull a whole fence to pieces.

Over the wire is a patch of bush. We crash through it, single file, wet ferns in our faces, branches of rimu and rata and kahikatea. The rain sounds different falling on the bush. Noisy. And then, through the branches, we all catch a glimpse of it, what we are here to see. I'm pretty sure Mum gasps. Dad says something, but I'm just silent, staring. As I said, it's not what you expect to see in a paddock on a dairy farm in the rain when you've been invited around for morning tea.

'They didn't want to leave it at the airport over the weekend,' Harry says.

'They couldn't leave it at the airport, you mean,' Di says.

'Worried something would happen to it?' Dad asks.

'They've been having a lot of problems lately.' Harry sighs.

It's big, I mean really big. It's white and has eight rotors and they're tied down to big stakes which have been stuck into the grass.

'It's impressive up close, isn't it?' Dad says.

'Certainly is.'

I walk around it, looking up at it, as I listen to them talk.

'I can't get over how huge it is,' Mum says.

'The lifting power it has is incredible. It can pick up several tonne at a time.'

'So they've hidden it on your farm? For the weekend?' Dad says.

'They did ask first,' Di says. 'Of course we said yes.'

'How many other people know it's here?'

'Just you, us, the helicopter pilots obviously. We gave them a lift into town afterwards.'

'You're not worried someone will find out, do some damage to the place? You are in the middle of nowhere out here,' Dad says.

'No point locking gates, is there,' Harry says.

'Annie, no Snapchat or Facebook or anything,' Mum calls out to me.

'There's no cell phone reception out here anyway,' Di says. 'And she's a sensible girl.'

'No, Mum,' I yell from the other side of the helicopter. It's so big I have to yell. I've heard about these helicopters, seen them the odd time flying high in the distance, read about how vandals have been targeting them. Although they're not vandals – they're not some kids with a spray can looking for something to tag. These are greenies, ecowarriors, whatever they call themselves. They think because they're saving the trees, and therefore somehow the world, they have the right to vandalise a helicopter. Loosen bolts that hold the rotors together, contaminate the fuel, endanger the crew. Peoples' lives are less important than a rimu tree that has been growing for hundreds of years and is now about to die anyway. The logging crews take the tree, lifting it out with the helicopter so no other tree is damaged in the process, and then they replant the area with more rimu trees. The light let in by the removal of the old tree revitalises the bush. It's completely sustainable. But the greenies want it stopped. Just like they want the coalmines closed. I don't understand it. Coalmining and logging means jobs, lots of jobs, and if there's anything the West Coast needs right now it's jobs. Sometimes it feels as if we're in the middle of a war.

Mum and Dad and Harry and Di have started back. Harry is leading us a different, quicker way. Obviously the dramatic entrance through the bush to the surprise is no longer needed. I run to catch up, hear conversations floating back through the rain. But it's not just rain – thunder is starting to rumble around the hills.

Di looks up, her expression worried. 'Just as well no one brought an umbrella,' she laughs, and we all quicken the pace. Thunderstorms are not something to be ignored here, not with all the trees.

At the house we all step out of our gumboots in the carport, and take off our raincoats, shaking the water off them. Inside, lights are turned on, the electric jug filled and plastic biscuit containers brought out.

'At least the power hasn't gone out,' Harry says. He takes a couple of logs, opens up the door of the woodburner, and feeds them in, sparks flying. Not that it's cold. It's just damp. The rain is loud on the roof, every few minutes the thunder a crescendo over the top of it.

'That one was close,' Mum says, frowning.

'Have some shortbread.' Di hands over a large container. 'Teas or coffees? Do you want a Milo, Annie?'

'Yes please.'

Everyone else is having coffee, the men with sugar, the women without, everyone has milk. The milk doesn't come in a carton, or a plastic throwaway container from the supermarket. Instead Di takes a jug out of the fridge. This milk comes from their cows.

We're sitting around their large kitchen table, which is in the centre of the room. The kitchen bench is along one wall, the fire on another, the TV with several couches circling it on the third. On the fourth wall is the door which leads to the rest of the house. Everything is crammed into the small space and everything is old, or cheap, or both. Dairy farming may make lots of money elsewhere in the country but here it doesn't, Dad has told me. With the rain, the cows don't milk as well, giving maybe half the production they would if they were in Canterbury. I asked him why the Browns farmed here and he said because this was where they lived and where Harry's parents had lived, and his grandparents. They carved the farm out of the bush more than a hundred years ago. Their great-grandchildren will probably still be battling the rain and the bush in another hundred years. Nothing will change. It's just the way it is.

The conversation slides from the storm outside to the milk price to what will happen if the coalmines close as biscuit containers are passed around and Di urges thirds upon us all. I don't have too much trouble resisting her chocolate mint slice. Nor does Mum, even after her chocolate binge yesterday. The heat from the fire and the room's wet fug is starting to make me sleepy, but talk of the explosion on our road and speculation about what has happened to Peter O'Shea wakes me up.

'They've brought in police from over the hill, I hear,' Harry is saying through a mouthful of ginger loaf. 'Some bigshot detective from Christchurch. He's staying out at the Cape, at Barney's Lodge. Has a fancy horse or something, so can't stay here in town.' Harry has a large face and equally large hands. The slab of ginger loaf doesn't have a chance. He could swallow it whole if he wanted to.

'Probably thinks we still ride horses over here to get around instead of driving cars,' Di adds.

'You don't really think Pete has done anything wrong?' Mum asks.

'Besides blowing up his house?' Dad replies.

'It was his house, he could do what he wanted with it.'

'I don't think anyone is allowed to blow up a house, whether they own it or not,' Dad says. 'Especially if it's surrounded by police.'

'If you mean do we think if Peter murdered this guy like they say he did, then the answer is no,' Harry says carefully. 'He hasn't got it in him.'

'He wouldn't hurt a fly, that kid,' Di says, draining her cup of coffee. 'Anyone else want another hot drink? Annie?'

'No thanks.'

'Remember when his dog died last year?' Harry says.

'No, I didn't know the dog was gone,' Mum says.

'About June it was. It was poorly, was off its tucker, was old. They didn't have the money to take it to the vet, so Pete brought it round here. He couldn't shoot it himself. Said he'd never killed anything. Didn't want to start. He couldn't even watch me do it. Then he took the body back home, probably buried it in the garden. I offered to bury it here, but no, he wanted to do it himself.'

'Poor boy,' Di says.

'Whatever the cops want him for, they've got it wrong.'

11

The thunderstorm hasn't stopped. Heading home, Dad has the car's headlights on and the wipers going as fast as they can and it's still not enough. At one point he just stops the car in the middle of the deserted, narrow road, unable to see, until it slackens off enough.

'The way it's going, we could have a flood,' Mum says, almost having to yell above the noise to be heard. She's peering up at the sky through the windscreen. Cocooned in the gloom of the back seat, I think about Barney's Lodge. I've heard of it, but never been there. It's in the bush somewhere, or by the beach at the Steeples, behind the Cape Pub. There are a lot of homestays, B&Bs, that sort of thing out there. So why didn't I butt in and tell Harry it wasn't the dad who had the horse, but his son? Why didn't I tell them everything, say I had met him on the beach, that we'd ridden together, that we had talked? That it wasn't a fancy horse, it was a quarter horse. A rodeo horse. Was it because Jack had kissed me?

But then, not telling people the truth seems to be what I'm doing a lot of these days. I made my school lunch in front of my dad and left it in Blue's feed shed and didn't say a word. And I got Blue to scuff out Pete's footprints, right in front of Jack, and didn't say anything then either. All those times I haven't lied. I just haven't told the truth about what I've been doing, what I know. Is that the same as lying?

Maybe the rain is beginning to get to me already.

Dad has started driving again – it hasn't eased off, he's just sick of waiting. We crawl along the gravel road that is starting to look more like a river. Lightning snakes across the sky for an instant, then the mountains roll with thunder seconds later.

'I don't think you should be taking Blue out this afternoon,' Mum calls back to me. 'He doesn't like thunder-storms, does he?'

'No.'

'It'll be over soon,' Dad yells. 'Never know, we might have a sunny afternoon.'

But by the time we get home the storm has gone out to sea and a fine mist has taken its place. I help Dad pull raincoats and gumboots from the boot of the car and listen again to Mum's demands to not tell anyone about the logging helicopter. She cooks sausages for lunch, and eggs. Di had given her a carton of eggs from her chooks. They live in the hay barn and hang out by the dairy where the cows are milked. Halfway through lunch my phone vibrates in my pocket. Jack has texted one word: *Beach?* I text back: *One hour*.

'Who's that?' Mum asks.

'Someone from school. Homework,' I reply.

'That's your afternoon organised.'

'I can do it later. Might take Blue out first.'

'Well, you know where I'll be. Stripping wallpaper.'

The mist is still there as I saddle Blue. There's hardly any point wearing a raincoat. This mist is the type that defies raincoats. But I wear one anyway, just in case the heavy rain returns.

Blue and I splash across Deadmans Creek, not getting any wetter than we already are. Deadmans is called Deadmans (no apostrophe required, apparently) for a reason. Back in the eighteen hundreds when people were looking for gold, the body of a prospector was found upstream from here in the creek. He had been murdered, his head bashed in. The young man's friend was convicted of murder since he was found wearing his boots. The friend was hung in Nelson, although he said he didn't do it. Back then they hung people for murder, even if there were no witnesses and no evidence except for a pair of boots. Still, brilliant name for a creek.

Jack is doing sharp turns with Tassie, but quickly falls in beside me and Blue in a slow canter.

'Are we still looking for a body?' he asks, taunting me with a smile.

'Unless you've heard they've found one.'

'Not that I know of.'

'Does your dad talk much about the investigation?'

'Sometimes.'

We've slowed to a walk. 'Meaning?'

'Sometimes he talks about it, sometimes he doesn't. So what did you do this morning? What do people do here when it rains all the time?'

'Visited friends with my parents.'

'Fun?'

'It was okay.' We ride in silence for a bit, then I finally find the courage to ask something I've been thinking about. 'Are rodeos cruel?'

Jack meets my eyes, then looks away, suddenly grumpy.

'It's just that some people say they are,' I add. 'That they kill horses.'

'Are you an animal rights campaigner? I didn't think you would be.'

'I'm not. I've just never been to a rodeo and that's what everyone says.'

'Horses do die, but so do the riders. Things happen. But then Blue could break a leg on this beach if he hit some soft sand, and he'd have to be put down. You could be thrown and break your back and have to spend the rest of your life in a wheelchair. Or worse, you could be knocked unconscious with the tide coming in and you'd drown.'

'Except you're here and I would like to think you would rescue me before that happened.'

'And if I wasn't here?'

'It all sounds a bit dramatic.'

'But it's all stuff that could happen, that has happened to people. Don't get out of bed in the morning – then you'll be fine.'

'Can we get back to rodeos?'

'What do you want to know?'

'It's not good for the animals, is it?'

'The horse that did my shoulder in walked away just fine. People say that rodeos stress animals, that the gear we use makes them buck, that it's not natural, but they don't know what they're talking about.' He's speaking with passion now. 'Horses buck in a paddock all by themselves – they're just having fun. You should see them in the arena. They get all fired up and buck you off, then prance around in front of everyone clapping and cheering, and then they go back into the pens quiet as anything. They know what's expected of them and they do what they've been taught to do. If they didn't like it, they'd be breaking pens and all sorts of things out the back. People don't see that. They just think they're watching this wild, untamed animal doing something it doesn't want to do, but it's all show. You should go to a rodeo one day. You'd like it.'

'Could I enter in the barrel racing?'

'If you're any good.' He sighs. 'You want me to teach you, don't you?'

'You don't want to?'

'I've just been wondering when you would ask. It's usually what most girls say in the first five minutes of meeting me.'

That makes me stop and think but Jack is already pulling Tassie up, getting off, waiting for me, holding out the reins. I don't hesitate anymore and do the same. I try to check the stirrup length on Tassie's saddle but the western set-up confuses me.

'They should be okay,' Jack says, seeing what I'm doing. 'I think our legs are about the same length.' I glance at him and realise that while I've been sizing Tassie up, he's been doing the same to me.

'Do you need a leg-up?'

Now he's pushing it. It's the standard joke – the only reason boys say that to girls at pony club is so they can get close to them. I roll my eyes at him, not that he seems to notice.

'I think I'm fine.'

He steps back, a smile still on his face. He's holding Blue loosely, one arm simply looped into the reins, his hands on his hips. Blue looks perfectly at ease. Tassie seems far from it.

I gather her reins by the saddle pommel, put my foot into the oversized western stirrup and haul myself up. As soon as my butt touches the saddle, Tassie does this pig jump with her back legs and I'm off, sitting in the sand.

By the time I figure out what has happened, Jack has grabbed Tassie and is laughing his head off. Blue doesn't even look concerned.

I get up, trying to brush the wet sand off my pants.

'You okay?' Jack asks, still laughing.

'Was that something you and she planned together?'

'Not a lot of people ride Tassie. I should have been holding her, making sure she behaved. I'm sorry. It's just that it was pretty funny to watch.'

'I'm sure it was.'

'Are you okay?'

'I'm fine.'

'Look, I'm sorry. I am.' He comes closer, pulling Tassie and Blue with him. 'Tassie, that was very bad,' he tells the horse, rubbing her nose, then he turns his attention back to me, laughter going from his eyes, replaced by something else.

Suddenly we're corralled by the two horses, safe from anyone watching, if anyone is watching on this beach on this wet afternoon, and he leans forward. I'm up against Blue's withers, my horse warm behind me, both sets of reins still in Jack's hands and I feel Jack's lips on my cheek, then finding my own, ready for him. Soft, hardly a touch, his mouth opening against mine. Then he pulls back, looking away, frowning into the rain.

'We shouldn't be doing this,' he says.

'Because you have a girlfriend?'

'Because tomorrow or in a couple of days or a week or a couple of weeks at the most, the investigation will be over and I'll be gone.'

'This is the West Coast,' I tell him. 'Anything can happen tomorrow. We take what we can get today.'

Jack looks at me, his eyes softening again. He bends down once more but this time his lips are on mine hard and urgent. I lean back against Blue, my head tilted upwards, and our mouths open and his hands are in my hair, holding my face. The rain runs down our faces and we're drinking it in, each other in, and there's the smell of wet horses and saddle leather and the sea and the wet bush and each other.

He's probably done this a thousand times before, with Stella, with other girls, rodeo girls, so I let him teach me. Does he realise that this is my first time, apart from the nose bump the other day when we were both on our horses? Does he understand that he is showing me what to do, how to do it? If he does, there is no sign. When he breaks away from me he is breathing hard, head down, forehead against mine, wet hair against my wet hair, hands still against either side of my face. I can feel the calluses on his fingers and palms, from bridles, from horses. Jack is no boy from school. He's a cowboy, a famous saddle bronc rider, and I'm just a girl on a West Coast beach in the rain riding a hack. Kissing a boy.

'Annie,' he says, then falters. We both just look at each other. He has no words to say any more than I do. What do I want to say? Kiss me again, make me feel like that again? Make this moment last forever? Stop time?

The horses are as still as we are. Maybe time has stopped.

'I need to get Tassie dry, out of this rain,' he says finally. 'She'll get cold.' He passes Blue's reins to me and then is on Tassie, already heading down the beach to where his vehicle and horse float are. He doesn't look back.

Blue and I watch them go, the black horse with its western saddle, the rider in his dark jacket, his short hair slicked back by the water. We watch them until they disappear into the rain and then I jump on Blue and we slowly turn to wade back over Deadmans.

Blue whinnies. I know he's complaining. Not much of a ride today, he's saying.

'Maybe tomorrow,' I answer.

12

But there's school tomorrow, not that I'm there long. I'm in the middle of maths, first period, when one of the office women arrives and tells me to come with her. I stuff my things into my bag and follow her out of the building, under the walkways which shelter us from the rain and to the school office where there is a policeman waiting, looking at the pictures on the wall. I don't pay him much attention, thinking I've been summoned for something else (did I forget a dentist appointment?).

'Annie, could you come with me, please,' he says, turning towards me. I recognise him. He's the one who stood guard outside our house after Pete blew up his house and the TV reporters kept bothering us. At least everyone is in class and not watching me getting put in the backseat of a police car for the five-minute ride across town to the station.

I want to ask him what's going on because I'm thinking of everything bad from a car accident (Mum), a train accident (Dad – he's on morning shifts now) to the police knowing somehow about me giving Pete my school lunch, but I'm too afraid to ask. He doesn't say anything, not the whole way.

At the station the cop pushes door codes and I'm past the public waiting area into a corridor. He gestures me through an open door, and I'm expecting it to be an interview room with a one-way mirror just like in *CSI* or *Criminal Minds* or *SVU*, but instead it's someone's office. Files and paper are stacked on a desk next to a computer screen along with telephones and other stuff. A blue-and-green striped tie is hanging off a cupboard doorknob and piled on top of a filing cabinet are disposable coffee cups with the Denniston Dog Café logo on them. The café is across the road.

And the window is new. The wood around the metal frame is unpainted as if someone has recently slotted it in, glass and frame. I look behind me and there are several small holes high up in the wall – shotgun pellets? Maybe this is the room Pete shot into that night. I'm trying to figure out how close the shot would have been if someone had been sitting at the desk, when a man comes in. He's wearing dark pants and a cream shirt, which is obviously missing the striped tie, and he looks about the same age as my dad.

'Sit down,' he says, pointing at a chair. By the time I sit down, awkwardly, my schoolbag still on my back, he's already in what appears to be his own chair behind the desk. He types something into the computer, using two fingers only, looking at the keys as he does so. Then he glances up at the screen and frowns, and that's when I figure out who he is. I've seen that frown before. Just brilliant.

'Annie,' he says, leaning over his desk to shake my hand. I have to stand up to comply. His grip is really firm, but I try not to show it. 'Sorry to pull you out of school. I hope you're not missing anything important.'

'It's okay,' I say, which it isn't. This is all far from okay.

'Jack told me last night how you'd seen something in the Orowaiti River Saturday week ago.'

I don't know what to call him. Jack's dad, or Detective Robertson, or what?

'It was just a raincoat.'

'What type?' He's pulled out a pad from under the rubble on his desk and is writing stuff down, his pen poised above the paper now waiting for my answer.

'I don't know, just a raincoat.'

'Black, red, green?'

'Black, I think. A dark colour.'

'And it was floating down the river, towards the sea? You saw it from the road bridge by the cemetery?'

'Yes.'

'About what time was this?'

'I was biking to basketball practice in town, so it would have been about ten to nine.'

'And it was just a raincoat? You didn't see anything else?'

'No.'

'There were no identifying features on the coat, nothing that you remember?'

'No.'

'How was it floating?'

'What do you mean?'

'Was it all wound up, was it inside out, you just saw the sleeves? Describe it.'

'It was floating hood first, down the river. I could see the outside of it. The arms were outstretched.'

'So like this?' He gets up and turns his back to me, stretches out his arms from his body.

'Yes.'

He sits back down, writes something on the pad, draws a picture. I can't quite make it out upside down.

'You could see the hood?'

'Yes.'

'And the current didn't swirl it around or anything?'

'It stayed just like that the whole way until I lost sight of it.'

'Anything else that you can tell me about it?'

'No.'

'You live down the end of Utopia Road, don't you?'

'Yes.'

He looks at me again as he's thinking about something. It makes me feel uncomfortable for some reason, the way he does it.

'Okay, thanks. You can go now. One of the cops at the front desk will take you back to school.'

He gets up as I do.

'It was nice to meet you, Annie,' he says and smiles again, and I try to return the smile.

It's interval when I get back, which means the whole school is there to watch me get out of the police car and walk to where my next class is. They all just stand and watch and then everyone is talking and I know there is only one thing they'll be talking about. Even the teachers on duty are all turning to each other and talking, their eyes still on me.

Mum rings exactly three minutes later on my phone. That's all it takes, three minutes, for the gossip to get across town from one school to another. From a high school to a primary school. English is just about to start, so I have seconds to tell her that I'm okay before my teacher growls at me and threatens to confiscate my phone. *No, Mum, you don't have to ring the police, I just had to answer a few questions about something I saw in the river. I'm fine.*

Which I'm not. I'm fuming.

Jack texts near the end of lunch: *I'm so sorry. Beach? Four?*

I don't text back.

On the way home (why didn't I bike today?) in the car, Mum's interrogation is nothing like Detective Robertson's. And we're following a very slow milk tanker, so the trip takes forever.

'They should have asked me to be there with you,' Mum says and I cringe inside at the thought. 'You are only fifteen. I still think I should ring them and complain.'

'They just wanted to know what I saw. I wasn't being convicted of anything.'

'It doesn't matter. And why didn't you tell us about this raincoat in the river?' Her voice is so loud I'm sure anyone on the footpath could hear her.

'I didn't think it was important.'

'So how did the police know that you'd seen it?'

'I don't know. Maybe someone in a car had seen me on the bridge at the time.'

'They didn't tell you how they knew? Didn't you ask?'

'Mum, the way gossip goes around this town, everyone knows everything, don't they?'

'Obviously not everything.' She adjusts the window wipers so they go slower. The rain is slackening off a little. 'You just should have told us. That day. When you saw the raincoat.'

The milk tanker has turned the corner into Utopia Road ahead of us instead of going straight. I sigh and stare out of the passenger window. Watch the graves in the cemetery as we pass them, think about how I can possibly answer her. How could I know seeing a raincoat floating down a river was important?

'So what are you up to this afternoon?' Mum asks before I can explain, her tone still the same.

'I was going to take Blue out.'

'You seem to be riding that horse a lot.'

'So? He gets fat if he doesn't get ridden.'

'It is raining, if you haven't noticed.'

13

Jack already has Tassie in a lather by the time Blue and I find him. The black horse stands there for a moment when they see us then Jack trots her up.

'I'm so sorry,' he says. 'I didn't know he was going to do that.'

'How did your dad even find me? You don't know my surname. You don't know anything about me.'

'He's a detective. How do you think he found you? How many girls are called Annie and go to school here and have a horse and live on Utopia Road?'

'Did you know he was going to do it? Why didn't you at least warn me?'

'I didn't know.'

'When did you find out?'

'I drove into town and had lunch with him today at that place across from the police station, and he told me then. He apologised, if it helps.'

'My mum is so pissed off with me.'

'You hadn't told her about the raincoat?'

'I haven't told her anything,' I yell at him as Blue shifts under me. 'It was just a raincoat. That's all I saw. What has it got to do with anything?'

'You don't get it, do you?' Now he's yelling too. 'It wasn't just a raincoat. It was a body wearing a raincoat. You saw the guy who was murdered that morning.'

'It was just a raincoat.'

'The police have been chucking raincoats into that river all morning after my dad talked to you, and none of them floated the way you described. The only way it would have happened is if someone was in it, face-down in the water, dead.'

I don't say anything, look away, up at Mount Rochfort surrounded by the rain clouds.

'You saw a body, Annie, and that's why I told him last night. Because I thought it was important – and it is. It gives them a timeline. It verifies the other witness' story about seeing the people dump it in the river upstream. It's all evidence.'

'So you can a pin a murder on my neighbour?'

'The guy who blew up the house and then escaped?

He's missing too, Annie. People don't just go missing. They've been trying to find him for days.' He stops yelling, seeing me fighting back tears. 'He's probably dead as well by now. I'm sorry. Did you know him?'

'Everyone knows everyone around here. Haven't you worked that out yet?' I press against Blue's sides with my knees and within two strides I'm cantering down the beach, angry at Jack, angry at myself.

A couple of minutes later there's the sound of hooves behind us. But Jack and Tassie stay back, they don't catch up, even though Blue slows slightly, wanting them to. But they just stay behind us, on the sea side. Blue tosses his head, telling me it's all my fault. I don't care. I look away from them, inland, at the washed-up driftwood and seaweed, still searching for a body. A body in a raincoat.

'Annie,' Jack calls from behind us. Blue stops and turns, even though I haven't told him to. 'I've got to get Tassie home.'

He's pointing up at where the sand meets the scrub line and there, on a gravel road, is a horse float and four-wheel-drive. Jack is already walking Tassie towards it and Blue follows, head down.

The horse float looks almost new. It's a double, able to fit two horses in it, and apart for some mud around the wheels is the cleanest float I've ever seen. Jack is already off Tassie and is lowering the back door. I jump off Blue and take Tassie's reins for him. Neither of us say anything. He starts undoing buckles on the saddle and heaves it off, carrying it into the float.

'You've got to dry everything here all the time,' he mutters, coming back for the saddle blanket. 'Some of Tassie's stuff is already going mouldy.'

I don't reply, just start trying to undo Tassie's bridle, but I'm lost with which parts come undone and which stay done up. Jack has it off in seconds and fastens a halter over Tassie's head in one practised movement. He clips a lead rope onto the halter and Tassie follows him up the ramp into the float. He doesn't even look back to see how she's going – it's like they've done it a thousand times before. But then, they probably have.

Jack comes out again and closes the back door of the float.

'Can we just sit in the truck and talk for a minute? Get out of the rain?' he asks me.

I nod. He has another lead rope in his pocket and he uses it to tie Blue to the back of the float, clipping the rope's end into the halter that I left on Blue under his bridle when I saddled him up, too lazy to take it off.

Jack disappears around to the driver's side. I take the passenger's.

The inside of the four-wheel drive is as clean as the float. Wet sand and mud are on the floor and a cardboard coffee cup from the Denniston Dog in the cup holder, but that's it. Not a chocolate wrapper or anything. Jack eases himself behind the wheel and looks across at me as I close the door.

'So do you have your full driver's licence?' I ask, to break the silence.

'I got it a couple of weeks ago. Dad got me to get it as soon as I could.'

'You're eighteen?'

'Seventeen and a half. That's the earliest you can get it, even if you have a cop for a father. When you turn sixteen, make sure you go get your learner's.'

I stare out at the rain through the windscreen, thinking about being old enough to drive, thinking about lots of things.

'Does your dad ride?' I ask, again breaking the silence.

'No, it was Mum. She taught us how to ride. All her side of the family are into rodeo. Especially my uncle. How about you? Do your parents ride?'

'No. I had to do the nagging thing to get Blue. And then it was just because he was offered to us. I don't think they would have ever gone out and bought me a horse but it was me or the meatworks for Blue. Mum didn't like the other option. I think Dad is still annoyed we had to get rid of the cattle so Blue could have the paddock.' Silence again. 'So what did he say about me? Your dad?'

I have to wait for Jack's answer. He's staring out at the rain as well. He's turned the key and is flipping the wipers on and off so we can see out of the windscreen. I'm keeping an eye on Blue in the rear-vision mirror outside the passenger window, or rather he's keeping an eye on me.

'He said you were very polite,' Jack says finally.

'Polite? Is that it?'

'Okay, and very nice.'

'Very nice?'

Jack sighs. 'Okay, you really want to know what he said?'

'Yes.'

'He said you were beautiful and that you were only fifteen and that I shouldn't break your heart.'

'I'm almost sixteen.'

'I know. You've said.'

'So what did you say to your dad?'

'I said you were the daughter of a West Coast coal train driver and you were tough and could take it and you were fearless on a horse.'

'No, I'm not.'

He gives me a sideways glance.

'The bit about the horse, that's all you're going to object to?'

'Can I object to the rest?'

'Probably not. You're steaming up the windows.' He hits a button and his window slides down but it doesn't help stop the windscreen from fogging up. He turns the heater on as well. 'Now the rain is coming in. Honestly, how do you live with this every day?' He brings the window back up.

'I should go,' I say, my hand on the door.

'Annie, you know I'm sorry about everything that's going on.'

I nod. He leans over and kisses me and I kiss him back. Suddenly it's like it's normal, expected, that's what we do when we leave each other, we kiss. I slide out of his arms, open the door. He starts furiously wiping the windscreen with his arm.

Mum and I are still not talking to each other by the time Dad gets home, although there's something else that's now taking precedence.

'There is a thing in the washing machine,' she says to him as soon as he comes in.

'What sort of thing?' Dad asks, taking off his jacket in the laundry. I'm stirring cheese sauce on the stove for tea and I have no idea what she's talking about.

'A thing that can survive the heavy-duty cycle, hot wash and washing powder. I was washing your overalls and it must have crept into them when they were hanging in the carport.'

'Is that why the juice container is on top of the washing machine?' he asks.

'It's the heaviest thing I had in the kitchen to stop it getting out.'

'Do I need a gun?'

'Maybe.'

I look from one of my parents to the other, trying to work out whether either of them is being serious and whether I should dial 111.

Dad takes the three-litre bottle of juice off the top of the washing machine, hands it to Mum, and slowly lifts the lid a fraction, peering inside.

'Kitchen tongs,' he says. Mum angrily slaps the tongs from the kitchen drawer into his hand as if he's a surgeon and they're forceps or a scalpel or something. Dad turns back to the washing machine.

'Got you!' He holds up the tongs for us to see. 'It's just a weta.'

The insect's legs are wriggling in the tongs. It's about the size of my hand.

'See its tusks?' Dad says.

Mum has a plastic container ready and holds it out to Dad at arm's length.

'See, real scary,' he says, trying to wave it in her face.

'Just put it in the container, please.'

Dad finally does what he's told and Mum slaps the lid on and passes it to me.

'You're the animal nut,' she says. 'Go find a nice tree for it to live in outside.'

'Okay,' I say, carefully taking the container.

'And far away from the house. I don't want it back inside,' she says, stirring the abandoned pot of cheese sauce.

I throw on a raincoat and take the container down to the bush on the edge of Blue's paddock. He comes over to see what I'm doing and snorts at me.

'Apparently they bite, so be careful,' I tell him, opening the container carefully and holding it up against the tree. The weta's legs scrabble uselessly against the plastic, so I have to half tip it out onto a branch, and then it's gone. Camouflaged perfectly.

I start to head back to the house but hear still-raised voices inside. This time they won't be about a tiny weta, they will be talking about me and my visit to the police station. Maybe I should just stay outside in the rain for a bit.

'You won't mind, will you, Blue?' I ask him. He whinnies back. *Get inside, don't be so pathetic,* he's saying.

Later on, after tea, when everything has finally quietened down (the cheese sauce got burnt and was chucked out, so we had to eat the cauliflower without it – which was about as nice as the mood in the house), I'm sitting on my bed looking at Facebook on my laptop. Now that he knows my last name from his dad, Jack, surprise, surprise, has sent me a friend request. I will be his two thousand and fifty-sixth friend. I accept the request and check out his details.

Home town is Christchurch. No family members listed, no relationships. I scroll down his feed. There are lots of rodeo pictures – Jack with horses, with other cowboys, lots of great shots with dust and hooves flying, in New Zealand, Australia, the United States, Canada. And there are lots of pictures of a girl who can only be Stella. She's tall, blonde, dark-eyed and beautiful. Lots of photos of Jack with his arm around her shoulders, both holding up trophy saddles and belt buckles, smiling at the camera, happy together. I don't want to look anymore.

14

'So have you heard about the new guy in town?' Samantha asks me on the way to our first class for the day.

'What new guy?' I reply, rolling my eyes. Boys, or the lack of them, or the uselessness of them, is a favourite topic of conversation for Sam.

'The detective's son, the one here for the murder investigation.' She drags out the word *murder* as she ducks under the covered walkway. I follow her and the drips from the spouting splatter down my back.

'Who is he?' I play dumb.

'We don't know his name. Yet.'

'Yet?'

'Rachel and I are planning to go out to the Cape Pub tonight. Her sister's taking us. Apparently he and his dad have been eating there. They're staying at Barney's Lodge.'

'So, what, are you just going to go up to him and start talking?'

'Why not?'

'Isn't that a bit obvious? And maybe he doesn't want to be bothered. Maybe he's already got a girlfriend.'

'Who said I wanted to be his girlfriend? Anyway, maybe he's lonely and wants to meet some locals. He's our age, maybe a little bit older. And he's cute.'

'Cute?' Some younger kids jostle us going the other way, trying to keep dry under the walkway too. Sam glares at them.

'In a cowboy sort of way,' she says. 'Rachel said when she saw him he was wearing a cowboy hat.'

'Where?'

'It was a black cowboy hat. At the Cape Pub. He took it off to eat. Put it on the chair next to him. I mean, who does that?'

'So Rachel has already seen him there?'

'But she was too nervous to go up and talk to him. That's why we're both going tonight. Together, you know. Safety in numbers.' She pulls open the door to the classroom and the conversation is finished with.

All the way through English I think about texting Jack about it, but what would I say? *Don't go to the Cape Pub tonight?* And what would he say back? I'm also thinking about Pete. Jack had said yesterday that he was still missing. It's been five days now since he blew up his house and no one has seen him, except me, I suppose (although technically I didn't see him). So where is he? Where is he sleeping, how is he getting food to eat? His car is still sitting outside his house, destroyed by the explosion and the fire, but he could have hitchhiked to Canterbury or gone Nelson way, got a ride with friends. Somehow I doubt it, though. This is his home. He was born here; second, third generation, maybe more. He doesn't know anywhere else, he's never gone anywhere else. He won't leave. Not when they're looking for him. He'll be hiding.

So if he's still here, where would he go? If he had somehow planned the explosion, did he manage to grab a sleeping bag, a tent, a gun, beforehand? Maybe. If he shot up the police station around midnight and then went home, would he have had enough time to set the explosives, pack a bag, plan where to go? (English, we're doing persuasive writing, is dead boring.) But none of it makes sense. Pete wouldn't hurt anyone or anything, I remember Harry Brown saying that on Sunday morning. He couldn't even shoot his own dog when it needed to be put down, so why would he attempt to shoot a cop at the police station?

There's a lot of bush on the other side of the road from the beach. Up into those hills, Mount Rochfort. Dense bush. Bush where no one would find you.

I glance across the classroom at Sam, at her long dark hair, her perfect face, her lips with their unmissable trace of lip gloss, and wonder what she would say to Jack and what he would say back to her. Maybe I should just get up and walk over to her desk right now and tell her that his name is Jack Robertson and that he wears a cowboy hat because he is a cowboy. A real cowboy. But then again, why bother? Why bother at all?

When I get into the car with Mum after school, Jack is texting me: *Beach, four?* I brush my phone against my skirt, trying to dry the rain off it.

'Is that Dad?' Mum asks.

'No. Why would it be?'

'He wants you to go with him this afternoon. Through the gorge. He's going to hold the train at Stafford Street for you. I'm taking you home to get changed out of your uniform.'

'Do I have to go?'

'When was the last time you did this together? When you were ten? Come on, this is special. You know it is.'

I text back to Jack that I can't make it. Mum and I don't talk the whole way home.

Dad is out of the engine talking to someone in one of the white trucks that service the line when we get there. He's got the train up by the railway crossing, still rumbling. Dairy cows are walking along a muddy track on the other side of the road, nose to tail over the railway line, on their way to milking. A few of them glance our way.

'Hello, pet,' Dad says to me, after ending the conversation with the man. 'Supervisor's not around so I thought we'd take the chance. Climb on up.' As Mum drives off I do what I'm told. The door is already open above me.

Being in a train is nothing like being in a car. For starters you're really high up and the seats are big and there are no seatbelts. If there's going to be a crash, drivers are supposed to lie flat on the floor, whatever that would do to save them. Dad has never had the chance to try it out, which I'm quite glad about. Not that he hasn't had accidents. Besides the Brown's cow, he's hit a car or a motorbike or something on a railway crossing most years, more accidents than truck drivers have. He always says that trains don't swerve to purposely hit cars. My advice: when you're driving, take a good long look both ways before crossing a railway line.

I'm in the left-hand seat. Dad has climbed up into the right-hand seat. The controls are in front of him but there are a few dials and stuff my side as well. No steering wheel, not like in a car. There's only one way to go, and that's along the tracks. Dad is looking out the window, watching the last of the cows cross the railway line. Behind them is a woman in a raincoat and waterproof leggings, wearing a helmet, riding a four-wheel motorbike. She gives us a wave as she crosses the tracks and then stops the motorbike, gets off and shuts the farm gate behind her. Dad waves back.

'I always watch out for those cows,' Dad says. 'They're pretty good though, haven't hit one yet.'

He pushes some buttons, pulls a lever and the train noise increases and we're slowly moving forward. The tracks are well above the paddocks, built up in case of flooding, and we're sitting pretty high as well, so we're looking down on everything. It's a great view. There are dairy farms and houses and patches of bush as the train starts to gather momentum and we head towards the gap in the mountains which is the start of the Buller River Gorge.

'This is Te Kuha,' Dad says. 'Used to be a hotel here, and houses and a ferry that took cars across the river, before they built the bridge at Westport. Now nothing is here. Nothing left to even show what was here once. So much history.'

Dad pulls the radio down and tells Wellington Control where we are. It's a safety thing. Every ten minutes he has to check in, just when we're in the gorge. If we miss the ten-minute call they come looking for us. It's one of only a few rail lines in New Zealand where the drivers have to do it, but then, being on this line, it's easy to understand why.

Going upriver the tracks are on the left-hand side of the gorge and the road is on the right. There's not enough room for both on one side. Even the road narrows to a single lane in places and in one area, at Hawks Crag, they had to blast the rock away to put the road in. On the rail side it's worse. The line seems to cling to the sheer cliffs and on a day like today the volume of water coming off them is massive. It's like we're driving through one long waterfall. However, the danger comes from the trees. Somehow trees grow up there on the sheer rock above the river, above where the train runs. If the water dislodges them, a slip, there is only one place they will go – onto the line. And with the track snaking around so many corners Dad wouldn't see a tree fallen onto the rails or the track completely gone until it was too late to stop. Or the trees, rock and everything else could all come down on top of him.

He's always said the beauty of the area, even when it's raining, makes up for the stress of driving through it. I'm not so sure. I'd rather have my dad around.

I look back out of the side window and see the train curving behind us as we chug over a bridge with a bend in it. Full coal wagon after full coal wagon follows us obediently in the rain.

'River's up,' Dad says. 'We could have a flood.'

The Buller is brown and swollen, eddies and currents churning the surface.

'So, have you thought about what you want to do, when you've finished school and everything?'

'Why?'

'Just wondering. Making conversation. You never seem to talk about it.'

'Maybe because I don't know. I'll probably stay around, find a job that I can do here. I was thinking of maybe working in the labs for the mines.'

'I don't think the mines will still be here, pet. Not by the time you finish school.'

'Something with the bush, then. Possum control, looking after the tracks.'

'You could go overseas, university, anything.'

'I like it here.'

'What if we're not here?'

'What do you mean?'

'This isn't where we belong. We're just here because of my job.'

'But we've always lived here.'

'No, we haven't. We came here just before you were born. You know that.'

'That's still kind of forever, Dad.'

'Might be for you, but it's not for your mum and me. And it's definitely not in West Coast terms. Remember, you have to have been born here to be a Coaster. Your mum and I are still imports. Always will be.' Dad's always said this in the past as if it's a joke. This time he's serious.

'So?'

'What I'm trying to tell you is that we have no ties here.'

'You have lots of friends here, lots of people you know,' I try to argue.

'We have friends everywhere, and anyway, you make new ones.'

I look out of the window at the bush, dripping with water. Deep green against deeper green, ferns and the hanging needles of rimu trees and the tiny leaves of the beech, the large, paler leaves of the broadleaves, of rata. And I think about Christchurch. The city over the hill, where all my cousins live and my aunts and uncles and my grandmother and friends of my parents. We go there a couple of times a year to visit, to go shopping, for weddings and funerals. There are streets full of houses and cars and tall buildings and traffic lights and noise. Brown grass, no rain, no green. Just heat in the summer, freezing cold in the winter. Snow and ice. The city where Jack Robertson lives, and his girlfriend, Stella.

'Would we go back to Christchurch if the mines closed? If you lose your job?'

'Maybe, probably. Depends on where I find a job, or where your mum finds a job. But yes, that's what we're thinking.'

15

Dad stops the train at Inangahua Junction, at the end of the gorge, his shift for the day ended. Another driver takes over. We're to take the car the other driver has brought up from Westport. I wait inside the car out of the rain while they talk briefly, then Dad climbs in, pushing the seat back. He's taller than the other driver. He flicks on the windscreen wipers and headlights and we drive back through the gorge, on the road side this time.

Mum has spaghetti and meatballs ready when we get home. And garlic bread, which is pretty good. She asks how the trip went. I say something enthusiastic about how much I loved it, about how great it was, because that's what she wants me to say, what Dad wants to hear. I know now that it's probably the last time I will ever ride in the engine of a train through the Buller River Gorge. It's probably the last time I will ride in the engine of a train with my dad. I figured it out in the silence on the way home in the car. I should have figured it out earlier. That's why Dad had wanted to take me, why Mum had wanted me to go.

After tea I see Blue, throw him a slab of hay. He neighs and snorts at me, complaining that he didn't get a ride today, that he didn't get to see Tassie, but he eats the hay anyway. There's only one thing he really cares about and that's his stomach. I go inside and help Mum strip more wallpaper off the hall walls.

'Don't you have homework to do or something?' she asks.

'This has got to be done,' I answer. And that's the end of the conversation. She has got one side finished, and we've moved on to the other. We work away quietly, listening to the TV in the living room and Dad snoring (not quietly) in front of it.

Jack texts me halfway through the evening and I have to stop, knife poised, ready to rip a huge section of wallpaper off in one hit.

Do you know a Samantha?

Why? I text back.

How dangerous is she?

Very.

Thanks. Missed you today.

Don't tell her that you know me.

Why?

Promise.

Okay.

I put the phone back in my pocket, not sure whether I can trust him or not. I'm trying to imagine what's happening at the Cape Pub. It would be funny watching Jack texting me while he's talking to Sam. She wouldn't have a clue. If only I could be sitting in a corner, behind the pool table, watching it all. Listening. It would be hard not to laugh out loud. But then again, maybe Jack will like her.

I get the full story the next morning at school, but I have to ask for it.

'So what happened?'

'What do you mean, what happened?' Sam replies.

'Last night, you and Rachel were going to go to the Cape Pub to meet that guy in the cowboy hat. Was he there?'

'He was there.'

'So?'

School hasn't started yet. We're in a classroom, because the rain is pretty heavy outside. Sam is sitting at a desk; I'm perched on the windowsill.

'So, what happened?'

'He said he has a girlfriend.'

'Bad luck,' I say, trying to sound disappointed for her.

'I know. He was still really nice, though. His name's Jack. Jack Robertson. We talked lots. He wanted to know about school and people and what's what.'

'I bet he did.'

'What do you mean by that?'

'I don't know. He's just someone from away. Probably thinks we all live in the bush or something.'

'He was really nice. To Rachel too, and her sister.'

'Was his dad there?'

'Yep. He was nice too. He left early, as soon as they'd finished eating. Jack said something about him having lots of work to do.'

'But Jack hung around talking with you?'

'He bought us a few drinks, just orange juice and stuff. Although we said they would serve us alcohol, he didn't want to buy it. We played a couple of games of pool. He was really good at it.'

'I bet you he was.'

'Why are you being so negative? Really, you should get out more. You know, do stuff. Meet people your own age. You should have come.'

'I was busy.'

'Maybe next time?'

'I thought you said he had a girlfriend.'

'So? We can still go and talk to him. She wasn't there giving us the evils or anything. It was a fun night. Next time you should come.'

On the beach, after school, Jack questions me if it was a set-up or not. Unbelievable.

'No, it wasn't. She'd heard about you – everyone is talking about you, by the way – and she wanted to meet you. I couldn't tell her *don't do it*, could I? That you already have a girlfriend?'

'Why not?' he asks, adjusting a buckle on his saddle as we walk the horses on the sand just above the waves.

'Because then she would know that I know you.'

'And what would be wrong with that?' He puts his foot back in the stirrup and looks at me.

'You really have no idea about how people love to gossip in this town, do you?'

'No, I don't. You know, you have a lot of photos of Blue on Facebook.'

'So?'

'Most people have photos of their friends, their family, you know, themselves.'

'Blue is family.'

'And you have only, like, forty-four friends. I am your forty-fourth friend. I don't think I know anyone who has as few friends as you do on Facebook. Except my grandmother, maybe.'

'I have a policy. They have to be real friends. Not just anybody. I have to know them and really like them and anyway—' I'm interrupted by him taking his phone out of his inside jacket pocket and checking it. I wait.

'It's from Stella. She came second,' he says excitedly. 'Second in the barrel racing.'

'Is second good?'

'Really good. She's pretty ecstatic.'

How he can tell someone on the other side of the world is ecstatic in a text is beyond me. And Tassie shows no sign of being ecstatic about the news, or even that she cares. Jack texts something back, then puts his phone in his pocket, but pulls it out again.

'It's Dad. Wanting to know if I'd heard Stella got second.' He sighs, busy texting.

'Sam said something about your dad being really busy,' I say when he finally puts his phone away, wiping the rain off it first with the inside of his jacket.

'He is, with this murder. It's got them worried, and there are no leads. You seeing that raincoat has been the only real break so far. One man dead but no body; one man on the run, and no one's seen him. For a town where supposedly everyone talks, no one is saying very much.'

'They're still searching for Pete, the guy who blew up the house across the road from us?'

'Dad thinks he's connected somehow. Maybe he helped in some way with the murder. They don't know. But they want to talk to him, make sure he's okay at the very least. That he's alive.'

'So have they checked his bank accounts, like they do on TV?'

'Dad said he hasn't used them. There's nothing.'

'So who actually got murdered?'

'They don't know that either. They just have this witness account of a body being dumped in the river and your neighbour freaking out about something, so freaked out he shot up the police station and then blew up his house – and there's a whole heap of explosives missing too.'

'Which were used to blow up the house.'

'But not all of them. And how did your neighbour even get them, let alone know how to use them?'

'I don't know. I didn't know him that well. I thought you said your dad didn't discuss his work with you much.'

'He's starting to, with this case. I think he's hoping with me getting to know people here, someone might tell me something that could help.'

'Like me and the raincoat?'

'It's such a small community, someone must know something.'

'I don't know anything else.'

'But if you did, you would tell me, wouldn't you? At the moment they're looking at all the employees at the coalmine, all those who have explosives knowledge. There've been a lot of people laid off over the last year there, they're talking to them as well. That's why he's so busy, which, really, I don't mind at all.'

'Why not?'

'Because it means I can keep staying out here with you, of course.'

'Don't you have schoolwork to do or something?'

'Don't you?'

I give Blue a good brush when we get home, thinking about Jack. It's beginning to be quite hard not to think about Jack. He kissed me again, when we left each other on the banks of Deadmans. And he had a look on his face, of longing, of sadness, which I know I can do nothing about. I get that he's missing Stella, especially after getting that text from her, that I am some poor substitute for her. At least I know now from Facebook that I don't look like her: I look nothing like her. I felt like saying, when he gazed at me that way, something like *she'll be back soon* or *I know you miss her* to make him feel better. But it would be nice to be her, to have Jack as a boyfriend. I wonder if she will ever know about me. His nobody, the girl who rode with him on the beach in the rain, the girl who fell off Tassie, her horse. What would it be like to be Stella – travelling the world competing, being so stunningly beautiful, having an amazing boyfriend?

I move to the other side of Blue, giving him long strokes across his back, and my mind drifts to what Jack said about his dad's investigation. If Pete hasn't used his bank accounts since he went missing, does that mean he's dead? Or does he have heaps of cash and doesn't need to use them? Or maybe he's gone somewhere where he can't use them, doesn't need to use them. Maybe somewhere where there are no money machines, no EFTPOS. I look over Blue's back to where Harry and Di's farm is, and then up at the mountains, at Mount Rochfort, and wonder.

Would Pete have the knowledge to survive in the bush? And for how long?

♦ ♦ ♦

That evening, I help Mum strip wallpaper again. Dad's gone out somewhere so there is just the two of us working away with Thomas the cat watching. We don't talk, there's just the sound of wallpaper tearing into tiny, tiny pieces and the rain drumming on the roof. Mum has already said she's booked the plasterer to come next week and the painter the week after that, so we will have to be finished by then for all of that to happen so we don't stop, even when we are both sick of it.

16

'So are we going to keep doing this, you know, horses, beach, rain thing?' Jack asks.

It's Thursday afternoon and apart from my Tuesday rail trip with Dad through the gorge we've been riding on the beach every day now since Friday. A whole week.

'What do you want to do?' I ask. We're heading towards the Whareatea River at a walk on the hard sand. It's almost low tide and the end of the waves spread out beneath us, all white froth. The horses' heads are up, ears constantly moving, listening to us talk, listening to the sea.

'I don't know, something without horses and rain.'

'You still haven't taught me how to barrel race.'

'Maybe when it stops raining. Annie, can't we just do something different for once?'

'Like what?'

'Like go somewhere – a café, the movies? Somewhere where it's dry. Do whatever people do around here.'

'I've told you there's a problem with that.'

'What?'

'People would see us.'

'Why is that a problem?'

'You've met Sam and you have to ask me that? Believe me, she's not the only one who wants to go out with you. The whole town is talking about you and your dad and you don't think that's a problem if we're seen together? And you probably should warn your dad, too. Everyone seems to know your mum's died. They're out to get him.'

'He did say something about that.'

'You see? I'm not making it up.'

'I just think you don't want to be seen with me because you haven't told your parents about us yet.'

'And there's that.'

'So they believe you're out riding Blue every afternoon because you like the rain?'

'I do like the rain.'

He says something else but my attention is no longer on him. I pull Blue to a stop, looking around.

'What?' Jack halts Tassie as well. She doesn't like it. Both of the horses are acting up but it's not because we've stopped.

'Smell that?' I ask him.

'Stay here,' he says, and urges Tassie into a trot, heading her up the beach to the high tide mark.

It's not the first time I've smelt that smell. Last time it was a rotting seal. I don't think it's a seal this time.

I let my breath out slowly, trying to concentrate on the smell of the sea instead. Wait. Watch. Jack disturbs a group of seagulls among the driftwood. They fly into the air shrieking at him. He turns Tassie around, his face suddenly pale, and trots back to me. 'Stay here,' he says again and unzips his jacket, reaching inside. Blue is jumpy, not wanting to keep still, and I turn him in a slow circle to settle him down. We both want to get away from the smell. We know what it is. I try to breathe through my mouth but it doesn't help.

'Hey, Dad, it's me. Yeah. Look, I think we've found a body on the beach.' Jack looks up at me. 'Yes, she's here. She hasn't seen it. I kept her away.' He listens again. 'Thanks, I was hoping you'd say that. But how about, you know, counselling and all that stuff? If she's not a witness, she won't be able to get it?' Eyes still on me. 'Okay. Ten minutes. I'll be by the float. You know where I'm parking it? See you soon.'

I finish another slow circle on Blue and look around at Jack.

'Annie, Dad has to send out the cavalry and if you're here you'll have to give a statement and ...'

'I know.'

'So you've got to go now.'

'What if it's Pete? I want to find out if it's Pete.' I push Blue towards the smell, towards where the seagulls have gathered again, hovering, landing on the sand, wings still spread, their necks outstretched, screeching.

'No, Annie. Don't do it.'

'I want to find out.'

Jack wheels Tassie round so he's blocking me. Blue stops, confused, unwilling to push past the black horse.

'I'll text you as soon as I find out if it's your neighbour or not,' Jack's saying. 'I promise. There's no time. You've got to go.'

'I just—'

'I will ring you, I promise. I love you.'

I nod, bite my lip, unable to speak, and turn Blue again. He takes a few reluctant steps but I kick him hard and we're in a gallop back down the beach, towards Deadmans, the rain coming down on us hard. I don't know if it's tears in my eyes or rain filling them up so much that I can't see. Does it matter?

Mum is stripping wallpaper again when I get into the house. She's multitasking – a casserole in the oven for tea, *Millionaire Hot Seat* on TV, up loud so she can hear it from the hallway where she is standing on a chair with her knife. Tiny pieces of wallpaper are falling onto the carpet below her like confetti.

'A,' she's yelling, 'the answer is A. How can they be so stupid on this programme?'

'Mum?'

'Annie, tea will be ready in about five. Could you get some plates out for me? Dad should be home any minute.'

I go back into the kitchen, hear the person answer D on the TV with one second to spare – they're wrong, the answer was A. Applause follows anyway.

'That was Dad driving in,' Mum says, washing her hands behind me in the kitchen sink. 'Let's dish it up.'

My phone is vibrating in my pocket and I pull it out, Mum glancing over at me, spoon poised halfway between casserole dish and plate. I quickly check it. There's a text from Jack: *Not your neighbour, will ring later.*

I text back: *Thanks.*

'Who was that?' Mum asks, concentrating again on the casserole.

'Just Sam, basketball stuff,' I answer, putting my phone in my pocket, rummaging for knives and forks in the drawer, trying to stop my hands from visibly shaking.

Dad comes in, shedding his jacket in the laundry in time to take the plate of food handed to him by Mum, and we sit down to watch the TV news, our plates on our laps. The casserole is Mum's usual, with baked potatoes, but I'm having trouble eating it. I chew the meat over and over but I can't swallow. It tastes like dust. About halfway through the latest update from Syria, Dad mutes the sound.

'They're going to let us know early next week who'll be laid off,' he says.

'How many?' Mum asks.

'They're not saying. Union is guessing it could be up to half of us.'

'But the mines aren't closing yet. Are they? There's been no announcement.'

'They're not closing but there are not the volumes anymore. Less coal going over the hill means fewer train drivers needed.' His voice is flat, like what he's saying is inevitable.

'Do you think it will be you?'

'I don't know. They used to have this first-on, first-off policy but all that's gone. Everything's changed. Nothing is the same as it used to be. Everyone is worried. Everyone thinks it will be them. Everyone's in the same boat as us.'

'Early next week?'

'We should know by then.'

Listening, I put another forkload of casserole into my mouth. If they expect me to say something, comment, my slow chewing excuses me. I can feel them both looking at me, both waiting. I chew even slower. They could have talked about this when I wasn't around, waited until I was in my bedroom doing homework. Then I wouldn't know anything, wouldn't have to wait and worry like they are. Maybe this is just another way of them letting me realise the situation, what is going on, so there will be no surprises, no shock.

Dad unmutes the sound. Syria is finished with and now it's milk prices. Another fall on the international market, dairy farmers worried.

'Poor Harry and Di,' Mum says.

'And now just in,' the TV news announcer is saying as the words 'Breaking News' flash across the bottom of the screen, 'we have reports of a body found washed up on a beach near Westport.'

'Turn it up!' Mum says, but Dad is already fiddling with the remote.

'A body was found late this afternoon on the Fairdown Beach just north of Westport on the South Island's West Coast, but is yet to be identified. Police are unable to say whether it is connected to the recent explosion which destroyed a local house, but hope a formal identification of the body will be completed by tomorrow. We will bring more updates to you as they come to hand.'

There's a brief shot of the beach in the rain, a police tent erected on the sand, people everywhere.

'Didn't you go riding on the beach after school today?' Mum says, looking at me.

'Yes, just by Deadmans. I didn't go far.'

'Didn't see any of this?' Dad asks.

'No. Didn't know about it.'

'That could have been you finding that body,' Dad says. 'You should be careful riding on that beach by yourself.'

I try to swallow more casserole and turn back to the TV, hoping my parents will do the same. There's something on now about an attempted bank robbery in Christchurch, explosives were used. Police have no suspects yet.

'I wonder who it is,' Mum says.

'Who?' Dad asks.

'The body.'

'Could be Pete's,' he says.

Mum shakes her head. 'I hope not. That would be awful.'

I manage, just, to scrape the last of the casserole off my plate and shovel it into my mouth. My parents have what they call a 'clean plate' policy: always finish what's given to you and then there are no arguments.

'I've got homework to do,' I mutter and carry my plate to the kitchen. If my parents reply I don't hear them over the noise of the TV. It's the sports news and then there will be the weather. I'm not missing anything. No need to watch the weather forecast for here.

Somewhere in the middle of my persuasive writing assignment for English my phone starts vibrating again in my jeans pocket. I'm lying on my bed, the bedroom door shut, James Bay playing on my laptop. It's Jack calling. I'd forgotten he was going to ring.

'Hi, it's me,' he says. 'You doing okay?'

'I'm fine.' I keep my voice low, just in case anyone is listening in the hallway.

'We've just got back.' I can hear a door shutting in the background.

'From the beach?'

'Yes.'

'It was on the TV news.'

'Was it?'

'My parents saw it.'

'Had you already told them?'

'No.'

'So did you tell them afterwards?'

'I couldn't.'

'Annie ...'

'My dad might be losing his job. They're laying off some of the train drivers. There's not enough coal coming from the mines to keep all the trains running.'

'Here, my dad wants to talk to you.'

I hear the phone changing hands.

'Annie, it's Grant Robertson, Jack's dad.'

'Hi.'

'I just want to make sure you're okay. Wasn't very nice on the beach today.'

'I'm fine.'

'People usually aren't fine after what you've been through.'

'Really, I'm okay.'

'We can offer you counselling. We can do it at your school, no one has to know. It can be completely confidential.'

'I'm okay.'

'If you change your mind, just ring me, or ring Jack. Anytime, you just ring, doesn't matter if it's the middle of the night. Anytime, okay?'

'Okay.'

'Here's Jack. I think he wants to talk to you again.'

'Hi, Annie. Look, I could come around. I could pick you up. I'll be twenty minutes. We could go somewhere. Anywhere you want to.'

'I'm okay.'

'You could tell your parents you're just going for a walk or something.'

'I'm okay.'

'You don't sound okay.'

I'm wiping tears off my cheeks with my fingers.

'I'm okay.'

'Annie?'

I turn the phone off. In the hallway I can hear Mum and her knife tugging at the wallpaper.

17

Brunner, Dobson, Strongman, Pike River. This is our litany, the West Coast's prayer for the dead. Our past. Our history.

Brunner, 1896, gas in the coalmine explodes after a charge goes off in the wrong place, where people shouldn't be, killing all of the sixty-five miners who are deep down in the pit. They get all the bodies out. Some are so torn up by the explosion they can only be identified by their clothes; others died of suffocation trying to escape. Thirty-three of the dead are buried in a mass grave at the Stillwater Cemetery. You can see the pictures online. They're black and white, of course. Two men standing in an open grave filled with coffins, a ladder behind them so the living can climb back out. Another photo with the same grave surrounded by people, sitting, standing, men, women.

Some must be standing on something so they can see over the others into the grave. There are even little kids peering in between legs. In 1896 there was no social welfare system, no widow's benefits.

Dobson, 1926, a gas explosion kills all nine coalminers in the mine. Two more explosions follow, hurling rocks from the mine's entrance onto people's houses nearby. In the end they have to flood the pit with water to put the fires out. The Municipal Band plays Handel's 'Dead March' at the funerals.

Strongman, 1967, a shot hole for a charge breaks through the face to an area where gas has built up in abandoned coal workings. It triggers an explosion. The abandoned workings should have been checked for gas, but they weren't. Two hundred and forty miners are down in the pit but a wet patch in the mine, where water seeps through the rock, puts the fireball out before it gets to most of them. Nineteen are killed. Fifteen of the bodies are found that day, but it takes three weeks to get to another two and the last two still remain there. They seal up the tunnel where they lie under the fallen rock. Five men who are part of the rescue team get the British Empire Medal for bravery.

Pike River, 2010, a methane gas explosion kills twenty-nine coalminers working about two kilometres into the shaft. Nobody knows what ignited the gas. Only two men make it out. They're about three hundred metres into the tunnel when it happens and are knocked off their feet by the explosion. Somehow they find each other in the smoke and the darkness and struggle together to the mine entrance. No one else follows, but for almost a week everyone hopes the twenty-nine men are still alive, in an air pocket, safe somewhere, somehow. For almost a week the whole country waits for the gas levels to drop, so the rescuers can go in safely. Everyone watches on TV. Then there is another explosion and then another until the coal is burning in the mountain and the shafts are collapsing. So they shut the mine, seal it – there is nothing else they believe they can do. Twenty-nine men buried in a mountain. My dad knows the father of one of them.

Brunner, Dobson, Strongman, Pike River – these are the ghosts that walk among us.

But not only the dead, the coalmines themselves are now becoming ghosts. Brunner, Dobson, Denniston, Strongman, Runanga and Pike River have all closed over the years. And maybe soon Stockton, where hundreds of people work, and from where my dad hauls the coal by train. Soon, with the downturn, there may be no coalmines left at all on the West Coast and more than one hundred and fifty years of history – of men going underground, of people taking off the overburden with diggers and trucks as big as houses to reach the black gold in opencast mines – will end. Our lives will be remembered in museums and on webpages. There will be no more heavy machinery on the coast, no more coal trains. The line will be empty, the sound of trains rumbling through the night gone forever. And the people will be gone too. There will be nothing left for them. What will the Coast be like then? Will there be only ghosts?

◆ ◆ ◆

On Friday after school I don't go to the beach with Blue. The rain is heavy. I'm sick of getting wet. I take Blue's cover off. It's giving him sores. His coat has bare patches. He runs around his paddock without it, mud flying, the rain soaking his back. And then he rolls around in the mud he's created like he's a pig, then trots back up to me and shakes his body all over and I have to step away or get splattered. Not funny, Blue. And no, I'm not going to brush you now.

Jack has been texting me on and off all day. Sam catches me replying at lunchtime and asks who it is, but I lie (why not? I'm getting good at it) and tell her it's my mum. *The body has been formally identified,* Jack texts, *and it's definitely not Pete.* It's who they thought it was (whoever that is – I don't ask). His dad has had to go to Christchurch, maybe for a few days – there's been a possible break in the investigation. *How are you?* He texts me that a lot. How am I?

Are you okay? Did you sleep okay? I lie to him as well. *I'm fine. Just fine.*

But I can't lie to Blue. If Dad loses his job and we leave and go to live in Christchurch, what will happen to my horse? We won't be able to take him with us. We can't sell our house (even if someone does want to buy it with its newly painted hallway) for enough money to buy one in Christchurch with a paddock for a horse. I don't even know if we'd have enough money to buy a house at all. Houses in Christchurch are a lot more expensive than here. I got Blue because he was going to be sent to the meatworks. Maybe I've just delayed his fate by a few years.

On Saturday morning there is basketball. The noise of balls against the court floor and our wet shoes squelching with every move we make gets to me. I'm off my game. I can't even shoot straight. Liam comes over to talk to me halfway through and we stand on the sideline of the court, watching the others as they run up and down.

'Annie, I heard they may be laying off some of the train drivers. I just wanted to say to you that I hope your dad will be okay.'

I nod.

'But whatever happens, you know, life goes on,' he says. 'Hey, look at me. I'm still here, I'm still doing what I love. Things will come right eventually. I'll get another job. The mines will start hiring again one day. So chin up. Be positive.'

I nod again and get back on court. A couple of minutes later Sam is by my side wanting to know what Liam was talking to me about.

'Nothing,' I tell her. 'Just stuff about shooting better.'

'You are crap today. I saw you miss before.'

After we finish up, Liam gets us all together and talks about the upcoming season. We'll soon start practising after school as well as on Saturday mornings, and in another couple of weeks games will start. We'll be travelling to games soon, and those games will be tough. Don't expect any of them to be easy, he says. He's talking to us, not at us, and we get it. This is serious. He's our coach and we are all he has. We can't let him down.

I cook myself instant noodles for lunch and avoid Mum. Jack has already texted me to meet him on the beach this afternoon, but I've texted back saying that I can't make it. I don't give a reason. The water boiling for the noodles makes the window by the stove steam up, but it doesn't stop me staring out of it. When I finally turn back to the pot the noodles have turned to mush. I eat a couple of mouthfuls while flicking through yesterday's *Westport News* which has been left on the dining table, but I don't read anything, just headlines. The rest of the noodles I chuck down the sink, run the tap and push them through the plughole with the fork until they're all gone. I grab my raincoat and dash out into the rain to throw Blue a slab of hay. He's grumpy that we're not going riding. He knows we should be, knows I've lied to Jack, that I've got nothing to do all afternoon.

'Well, some days are just bad,' I tell him. 'That's just the way it is.' Blue nibbles a corner of hay, then leaves it and canters around the paddock. He's saying *if you don't take me riding I'm going to mess up the paddock.*

'Go for it,' I tell him. 'See if I care.' And I leave him to it. I'm getting wet anyway.

18

Saturday afternoon, Saturday evening, Sunday morning. Jack texts: *Beach today, one?* I text again that I can't make it. He texts back that he wants to see me. I give up and text that I'll be there. Sometimes giving up, giving in, is easier.

About twelve-thirty, I put my raincoat on and go out and see Blue, brush him with a currycomb. He needs it – without his cover on he has turned into something more like a mud monster than a horse. He even has tangles in his mane. I spend a long time brushing him then get the saddle out. He's all excited after two days in his paddock, whinny-ing in my ear, snorting and stamping his feet.

'Stay still,' I tell him, doing up the girth. He's not making any of it easy.

And then I'm in the saddle and he's heading for the

beach without me even telling him, and that feeling of being twisted-up inside is back. The beach is the last place I want to go.

Jack and Tassie are by the driftwood tree. Jack is off Tassie, holding her by the reins, waiting for us in the drizzle.

'I didn't think you would come,' he says.

'Sorry I'm late,' I mumble.

'You don't have to be sorry. It's no big deal. Tassie and I haven't got anything else on this afternoon. Apart from a geography assignment which I don't want to do.'

'Geography?'

'I still do schoolwork, and Year Thirteen is no breeze. Anyway, I'm going to teach you how to barrel race.'

'Do I have to?' I ask. All I feel like doing is heading home, getting dry, curling up in bed in the dark and staying there. But I can't tell him that, not when he's standing waiting for me, hands on hips, ready.

'Yes. You wanted to learn and today is the day I'm going to teach you.'

'Tassie will just buck me off again.'

'No, she won't. I won't let her. And since when have you ever been afraid of a horse?'

I get off Blue, my face momentarily against his saddle where Jack can't see me, and quickly wipe the tears from my eyes. If he notices when I turn to him, he doesn't say anything and instead just takes Blue's reins out of my hands. I stand looking up at Tassie's saddle, put my foot in the stirrup and haul myself up. I wait, ready for her pig jump, half-hoping she will throw me off just like last time so I have an excuse, but Jack is holding her head, both hands on either side of her bridle. He looks up at me.

'Okay?'

'Yes.'

'So just walk her up and down the beach a little, get the feel of her.'

I do what I'm told. She's like a coiled spring, all energy waiting to be released. Blue is mud fat, I admit it. Tassie is so, so different.

'Keep the reins looser, use your legs more for cues,' Jack calls out to me. 'Try to turn her just by using your legs.'

I press against her with my left leg and, sure enough, she turns and we're back walking towards Blue and Jack. Blue doesn't seem the least bit interested in seeing me on another horse. He's using Jack's back as a scratching post for his head and Jack's letting him.

'Keep centred even more in the saddle,' he says as we stop next to him. 'It's really important in barrel racing. Sit tall but firmly down in the saddle and as still as you can as she goes round. That's better. You look good. What do you think of her?'

'She's different.'

'Ready to give it a go?' He nods at the driftwood tree. 'Just get around it, don't try to go too fast.'

'Which way round, left or right?

'You've got to do both on the course so whichever one. Just let Tassie know.'

I decide to give it a go at a trot, but Tassie has other ideas. She launches into a canter straight off, and if it wasn't for the western saddle horn I'd be on the sand wondering what happened. I panic and grab it with my right hand, my left flung wide and we've scooted around the tree before I've even realised. I only just manage to get myself back into the saddle properly by the time we're standing by Jack.

'This time, don't lean. Okay? Stay centred, let Tassie do the work. Don't take the turn for her.'

I almost say something about Tassie doing all the work, but keep my mouth shut and start her off again. The trot still doesn't happen, but this time I think more about my balance and staying centred rather than trying to slow down. And it's better. I don't have to grab the saddle horn. Jack nods his approval when we come up to him, so I turn her around and we try it again, this time just a little bit faster. I'm not sure if that's from me or Tassie. Maybe it was a joint decision.

'Should I be using both hands with the reins or holding them in one or something?' I ask as we halt again by Jack. Blue is watching the waves, totally bored.

'Both hands. You're doing great. Nice and quiet. Look more at the line you're going round the tree, not the tree itself. A horse will tend to go to where you're looking. You don't want her to crash into the tree.'

'I don't think she's that dumb.'

'I'm not saying that. It's about balance. If you're still and balanced, she can go faster without having to compensate for what you're doing.'

'I think we're going quite fast enough.'

'You can go a lot faster.'

He sends us off again and again, and he's right, we do get faster. A lot faster. I try going round the tree the other way and Tassie listens to me and does what I want. We're working together at last. Now I've figured out what is happening and where my arms and legs and body and, yes, eyes should be, I can actually watch what Tassie is doing, feel what she's doing. She's so supple and strong it's unbelievable. It's like she's turning on the spot.

'Okay, that's enough for your first lesson,' Jack calls out at last. Tassie's coat is wet with rain and sweat and I feel exhausted as well. 'I'd like to see how fast you would go on a proper course – we're not going to do that here.'

'How fast do they get up to?' I ask as I jump off, my legs feeling like jelly.

'Under seventeen seconds for three barrels. It's pretty fast in the top competition.' He takes Tassie's reins from me and gives me Blue's.

'Would I be that fast?'

'Well, first we'd need to get you a cowboy hat,' he says, smiling.

'And a horse. Tassie belongs to Stella,' I remind him.

'I think we could find you a horse, maybe not as good as Tassie, not yet, but we have a couple of young horses back home that need work.'

'Are you being serious?'

'I'm always serious, especially with you.'

'Now I know you're definitely joking.'

Instead of replying he pulls me closer and kisses me, his arms around my waist. My hands go to his neck, under his jacket, and I feel the strapping through his shirt, around his shoulder. It's thick.

'Does that still hurt?' I ask, pulling away, looking at his face. 'From the accident?'

'Sometimes. I was seeing a physio a couple of times a week before I came here.'

'Is it going to come right?'

'Of course it's going to come right. I'll be back in the saddle in no time, ma'am.'

'You still being serious?'

'It's going to come right. I'm going to be Jack Robertson, famous saddle bronc rider again.'

Riding back over Deadmans I feel happy, happier than I have for days. I glance back at Jack, but he's already turned around and heading to his float. Did he do all this on purpose? Make me concentrate on riding Tassie so I'd forget everything else for a while? Maybe. Probably. I don't know. It's worked, anyway. But my legs really ache.

At home I give Blue another good brush (he's still got mud all over him) and put him back in his paddock, this time with his cover on. He quiet, content too, even though he's had hardly any exercise. He just stood all afternoon, his reins over Jack's arm, watching.

Jack texts me about an hour later: *Geography is so boring*.

Try persuasive English writing.

Been there, done that.

So we're texting again too.

Watching the news and eating pizza Mum has made (it's not as if we can ring up Hell Pizza or Domino's, is it?), there's something about a bank robbery in Christchurch.

'That happened Thursday, didn't it?' Mum says.

I try to remember back to Thursday night and at the same time try not to let my olives slide off with the melted cheese. The robbery, the news announcer is saying, has been linked to an explosion just over a week ago in Westport.

'Pete's house?' Dad asks.

'Could be,' Mum says.

And then Jack's dad fills the TV screen, telling the whole country the explosives that were going to be used in the bank robbery (the robbery had been stopped by police before an explosion happened) were some of those missing from the Westport storage facility. They checked the serial numbers. Powergel has serial numbers on the packaging. I didn't know that.

'Who's that guy?' Dad asks.

I take a quick bite of pizza, although he's not expecting an answer from me. He's just thinking out loud: what has Jack's dad got to do with what is happening in Westport? But I do know the answer: everything.

There have been no arrests made, for the bank robbery or the house explosion or related to the body found on the Fairdown Beach, but they're *following lines of inquiry*, there are *certain people of interest*. I realise I've seen Jack's dad before on TV. Many times, for as long as I can remember, he's been the face for murder. He looks different than he does in real life. In real life he's taller, thinner. So it's just not Jack who's a celebrity, it's his dad as well. He's the go-to cop when something bad has happened – murders, explosions, bank robberies. So that's what he's doing in Christchurch, but why did he leave his son here for the weekend? Why didn't Jack go with him?

My phone vibrates in my pocket.

See my dad on TV? Jack must have been watching the news too.

Yep.

19

I'm still thinking about the bank robbery and the link to the missing explosives from the shed out on the pakihi while I'm getting dropped off to school the next morning by Mum. I don't know what she makes of my silence. But then again, she's not doing a lot of talking herself.

And the day steadily gets worse. It's a Monday, but even Mondays shouldn't be as bad as this. Mid-morning we're told we have a speaker to listen to in the hall. Everyone moans and then gets up as slowly as possible to walk to the hall in the rain. None of us want to cram in there, sitting on the uncomfortable forms, listening to someone drone on about their life story. Teachers think that because we are a small high school in the middle of nowhere, we need to be motivated, we need to know that whoever we are and wherever we come from there is still the chance that we too can be great. We've had All Blacks, netballers, the odd children's author, musicians, entrepreneurs, business-people. Some of them are faintly interesting, most of them are not. Then again, they might be if the forms in the hall were more comfortable. We have no idea who today's speaker is. Samantha, sitting beside me, is yawning already and it hasn't even started.

The principal is doing the usual stuff on the stage. The speaker must be sitting in the front row somewhere. My class is halfway back, so we can't see who it is, but finally someone stands up and climbs the steps to the stage. He's putting a black cowboy hat on his head.

'I can't believe it! It's Jack,' Sam squeals in my ear.

I slump down in the seat, or Sam sits bolt upright, I'm not entirely sure which, but suddenly it seems she's at least a metre taller than me. Her face is beaming, a 'look at me, look at me' glint in her eyes. The principal is still droning on with his introduction as Jack gets to the lectern. He's wearing a black shirt, the collar open, and blue jeans with a big silver western belt buckle that he must have won as a prize at some rodeo. As he waits patiently by the lectern, his eyes, under the brim of his western hat, are scanning all of us. It takes him a good minute to find me and smile that smile of his.

'He's smiling at me,' Sam leans down to whisper, her eyes never leaving the school stage.

I shake my head slowly at him, making the smallest movement required, aware of teachers' eyes on us. Jack grins back, then is interrupted by the principal inviting him to step up to the lectern.

'Um, hi everyone. I'm Jack Robertson. As your principal has just said, I'm a professional saddle bronc rider. I didn't know I was going to be speaking to you today until a couple of hours ago, so I haven't really prepared anything. I hope that's okay. I just thought I'd talk about what I do and why I do it and maybe make some of you think about getting into the sport that I love so dearly.

'I'm a Year Thirteen – hi guys.' He gives a wave to those sitting at the very back of the hall. 'I do school by correspondence, because I'm travelling so much, but if I'm going to be here a while I might come and join you. Looks like a pretty good school. You could help me with the geography assignment I'm struggling with at the moment.'

And then he starts talking about rodeos and bull riding and bareback and all of the rest. He's a confident speaker, like he's done it a million times before, and the school is hanging off his every word, gasping at the right moments, laughing at others as he tells stories about what he's seen, what has happened to him and to other riders. It's a Jack I don't know. He's the professional, the rodeo cowboy. The boy on the beach complaining about the rain is not this boy on the stage, enthralling even the teachers about saddles and the Cowboy's Prayer and roping and sweat and dust, here and in Australia and Canada and America. His eyes are constantly moving over us all, but they always come back to me, lingering on me, and every time he does it there is a quick smile, a look away, and then back again, curiosity as much as anything else on his face.

Sam can hardly sit still beside me.

After about half an hour Jack wraps it up, tips his hat to us, and everyone applauds. I think I go temporarily deaf from Sam's clapping. He walks down the stage steps and back to where the junior classes are sitting, lost in the crowd as we all get up. I sidle down the forms to the hall doors, hoping to escape, but Sam is blocking my path, trying to see where Jack has gone, waving frantically. And then he's right in front of me, shaking a few of the guys' hands on the way, saying the odd word here and there, but undeniably walking straight towards us.

'Jack, Jack, over here,' Sam calls out to him. Not that she has to.

He sidesteps the last person between us and Sam reaches up to kiss him on the cheek. The brim of the black cowboy hat, as black as Tassie's coat when it's gleaming with sweat, hides from me whatever his expression is as he kisses her back.

'Annie, I would like you to meet Jack Robertson,' she says formally, turning to me.

Jack smiles at me from under the hat. 'Nice to meet you, Annie.'

'Annie's one of my friends I was telling you about. She plays basketball with me.'

'Does she?'

'Oh, and she has a horse. You two have something in common.'

'Maybe the three of us could go out together some-time? Maybe have a meal?'

'I've got a lot of schoolwork,' I manage to get out.

'She's really busy,' Sam backs me up. 'And her parents don't really let her go out a lot.'

'Okay, maybe sometime, though,' Jack says.

'Can I take a picture of you and me, Jack?' Sam says, pulling out her phone.

'Of course.'

Sam holds her phone at arm's length and gets real close to Jack, smiles sweetly and takes the selfie.

'Thank you so much,' she tells him.

'My pleasure. It was great to bump into you again, but I'd better be going. And it was nice to meet you finally, Annie.' And then he leans over and kisses me on the cheek, his breath on my ear and I have to close my eyes.

'That's what cowboys do. They don't shake hands, they kiss you on the cheek,' Sam tells me as we watch him walk away. 'Isn't he amazing? Just think, he could be coming to study at this school!'

On the way to class, with Sam still talking about Jack, I get a text. *I've never seen you with dry hair*. I put the phone back in my pocket.

If I'm having trouble concentrating on schoolwork after that, Sam has it even worse. The rest of the day is a struggle. Classes, rain, Sam. In the end I start avoiding her. I can't handle watching her staring into the distance sighing all the time. She even asked me at lunchtime if I could possibly teach her to ride Blue. I told her that the famous international saddle bronc rider Jack Robertson would not really be interested in a girl who rode an ex-pacer. He would only be pretending.

'Perhaps I could tell him that Blue is a special horse or something?'

'I think he would know,' I say.

'Still.'

On the beach near Deadmans, Jack is still laughing about it.

'You're cruel,' I tell him as we start down the beach at a walk.

'I'm not being cruel. You've seen my Facebook page. There are hundreds of girls on it just like her.'

'I'd say more like thousands. Actually you have two thousand and something friends on Facebook.'

'They're not all girls, and anyway, they just think a rodeo rider is someone special. They don't know me, they don't know anything about me – what I think, what I want – but they're all falling in love with me just because I wear a cowboy hat.'

'Yet you still wear the hat.'

'Why shouldn't I?'

'So you do like the attention, don't you?'

'What's not to like?' He smiles at me again, and I know he's joking this time. 'Look,' he says, suddenly serious, 'if I really liked it, all those girls, would I be riding on a beach with you in the rain?'

I turn my head away, wanting to keep my thoughts to myself. But he's waiting for an answer. I kick Blue into a canter instead.

We race along the beach, the rain becoming heavier, the surf right at the horses' feet. It's as if the whole world is made of water. Waves, rain, sweat – they're all one. And tears.

Jack catches up with me.

'What I really won't like,' he yells out to me above the noise of the rain and the hooves on the sand, 'is when we can't do this anymore.'

I stop Blue and Jack pulls up Tassie. We face each other.

'Dad's back from Christchurch,' he says. 'They're setting up roadblocks in the Buller Gorge and on the Coast

Road. They're going to search every car that's coming or leaving Westport.'

'Looking for the rest of the Powergel?'

'Yes, and the people connected. It's nothing to do with drugs, like they first thought. It's bank robberies. They stole the Powergel to use in bank robberies. They know who they are, Annie. They're going to start searching houses, flush them out, make them run.'

'But what if they're just Westport people? People who have lost their jobs in the mines? People I know?'

'They're still murderers. That body on the beach – they're pretty sure that was your guy in the raincoat, the one you saw floating down the river.'

'Maybe it wasn't a murder. Maybe it was an accident?'

'The guy's head was bashed in, Annie. It was murder.'

'Then why dump the body like that? Why didn't they hide it so no one would ever find it?'

'I don't know, maybe they got scared. Panicked. Rushed it. Then that guy blew up his house.'

'The police had his house surrounded.'

'Whatever, Annie. It doesn't matter. In a couple of days all this is going to be over and I'll be leaving.'

20

Harry and Di are coming for dinner. It's a Monday night, but for dairy farmers every day is the same – the cows don't stop needing to be milked just because it's the weekend. And Dad has tomorrow off, so a Monday was decided upon. Mum has cooked lasagne with pasta she made herself (she got the pasta press thing through Fly Buys last year) using Di's eggs. I know it's going to be good, and it is.

We sit at the table, not eating tea on our laps in the living room as usual, and the TV is off. Tonight, talking to friends is more important than watching the news. And there's garlic bread too. Even better.

I've come in wet and smelling of horse, so explanations are needed. Blue needs exercising, even in the rain, Mum says to Di. I smile in agreement, grabbing a towel.

If only she knew. I can still feel Jack's mouth pressed onto mine. Dad and Harry are talking about whether the rivers are going to flood and then they move on to the milk price and oil and petrol prices and the mine layoffs and China and coal. They all seem to be mixed up together, or I'm just totally confused about the whole thing. China has stopped buying oil and coal so prices are falling, which means the countries that used to make lots of money out of oil and coal (pretty well every country in the world, it seems) can't afford to buy milk. Our milk. Or our coal. Just as well we don't produce much oil as a country. Three strikes and you're out.

Di passes me the broccoli as the conversation moves to Dad's job, or maybe lack of a job.

'What will you do?' Di asks.

'He hasn't been laid off yet,' Mum says. 'Let's wait for that to happen first. We'll find out tomorrow at the meeting.' And she smiles across the table at me and everyone shuts up. They understand. No talking about moving away in front of the kid. Honestly, I'm quite happy about that. I don't want to talk about it either.

Mum and Di discuss what colour to paint the hallway (off-white or cream or maybe pale blue?) and Dad starts talking with Harry about what happened when he was coming through the Buller River Gorge this afternoon on the train. He was watching the road on the other side and just at Hawks Crag police were stopping cars. He says it didn't look like a usual licence, warrant, rego check. They were getting people out, making them stand on the side of the road in the rain while they searched the whole car. They had dogs. It was holding up the traffic.

'Why would they be doing that?' Di asks, no longer talking paint colours with Mum.

'I don't know. Someone said when I got back they were looking for the missing Powergel. That the dogs could sniff out explosives.'

'They think someone is crazy enough to put it in a car and drive out of Westport?' Harry says. 'After what happened in Christchurch with that bank robbery?'

'There's only the two ways out, either through the gorge or down the Coast Road.'

'They're probably doing the same thing down there,' Mum says.

I sweep the last of the pasta off my plate with my fork as I listen.

'It's just crazy,' Harry says.

'If they are searching people's cars, they might start searching people's homes next,' Di says slowly.

Something about the way she says it makes me turn and look at her. Worry is on her face. This isn't a conversation about town gossip that is kind of amusing but nothing to do with us, that my parents and Harry and Di would laugh about together. This is different. I glance across the table at Dad, but he has his head down, concentrating on mopping up the sauce with the garlic bread. Mum has got up and gone into the kitchen to check on the apple pie, which Di has brought and is keeping warm in the oven. So there's just me and Harry and Di and Dad, and Harry and Di are looking at each other in this weird way and Dad is not noticing, still concentrating on his garlic bread.

'I'll take the plates,' I say, getting up quickly, picking up my own.

'Thanks, pet,' Dad says, handing his across. I grab Harry's and Di's and scoot into the kitchen. Mum is fussing about whether the pie is warm enough.

'Was the lasagne okay?' she asks.

'It was great.'

'So what's everyone talking about out there now?'

'Nothing much.' I'm rinsing the plates and stacking them in the dishwasher.

'I think this is going to be a few more minutes,' she says, still looking at the apple pie through the oven window. Which means she's going to stay standing in the kitchen and I'll have to go and sit down at the table again.

'I might just check an email then. My English teacher said something about sending us stuff and it hasn't come through yet.' Small, tiny, necessary lie to get me out of having to go back in there.

'Okay. Five minutes, no more?'

I head out of the kitchen and into the hallway, but Harry is already there. He has his back to me, his phone to his ear.

'Just go. Take whatever you need, don't worry about it. Just go,' he's saying, his voice urgent, hurried.

I back out quickly, end up in the bathroom, shut the door quietly. Hopefully he hasn't seen or heard me. Footsteps going past. He must have gone into the dining room again. So who was he talking to just now on the phone, and why are he and Di so worried about the police searching homes, maybe their home?

The apple pie is amazing (and at the perfect temperature to make the ice cream ooze off it as it melts) and with Mum at the table again the conversation has returned to paint colours and funny things that have happened in the office at St Canice's School and when it will stop raining.

'I've given up. I'm using the dryer,' Mum says. 'We were running out of clothes.'

'Can't have a rainforest without rain,' Harry says and, plates pushed aside, everyone gets up and heads to the living room.

'Annie, could you put the jug on for cups of tea?' Mum asks.

'Sure.' I grab plates to take out with me.

Jug on, dishwasher now so full I can't fit anything more in it, I look out of the window. It's grown dark and I haven't given Blue any hay. How did I forget to do that? I know how I forgot: Jack's kisses. This is getting bad. At least he'll be leaving soon with his dad and things can get back to normal. Even if the investigation does drag on, Stella must be due back from the States soon and then it will be all over. No more rides along the beach for Tassie.

I grab my raincoat by the back door and head out into the dark with a torch. Although I don't really need it. There's enough light around and I know where I'm going. I push open the feed shed door and grab a slab of hay.

'Hey, Blue,' I call out.

The sound of hooves in the dark. Neighing. I've turned off the torch, but he knows I'm there. He can smell the hay.

I toss it over the fence, feel his head press into my hand as he bends down.

'Sorry I forgot,' I tell him. He doesn't seem to care. He's munching steadily.

Something distracts me, a light, by Harry and Di's farm. The light is moving. As I watch, it crosses over to where the track leads up to Mount Rochfort. But why? Who was at the farm and is now heading up the mountain in the dark and the rain? There are no houses up there, just a lake and a small hydro scheme. The gates at the bottom of the road are always locked, but those aren't car headlights. Too small. Someone is heading up there with a torch.

21

Mum picks me up from school the next day as usual, but for once I don't get interrogated. There's no *so how was your day* or *what did you learn today* or *have you got much study to do tonight* or anything. Instead we drive in silence in the rain. Jack is texting me: *Beach?*

'Dad and I are going to a meeting after we get home,' Mum says.

'Okay,' I say, still holding my phone.

'About his job. They're going to announce the redundancies, who's getting laid off. I'm going with him. All the wives are. We could be late home.'

I nod and start texting on my phone.

And then we drive in silence, through town, across the Orowaiti Bridge.

'Everything is flooding,' Mum says.

I look out at the river. It's high, higher than I think I've ever seen it.

'The overflow will be working, the Buller pushing into the Orowaiti,' Mum says.

'Will the town flood?' I ask.

'The park by the Buller Bridge, that's under, but that always happens. This river here stops the town flooding.'

She turns off at the cemetery, along Utopia Road and then we're home. Mum hurries inside after she pulls into the carport. Jack has texted me back: *See you soon*.

After I've got changed out of my school uniform, seen my parents off, I wait for him in the carport, sheltered from the rain. I've already thrown Blue a slab of hay, just in case we're late back. Blue wasn't impressed – he wanted to go riding – but he still ate the hay as always. I can still hear him munching, even from here.

I step out from the carport when I see Jack's vehicle coming down the driveway. He's peering through the windscreen, looking at the house, at everything. If I was him I would be too. When he sees me he stops and gives me a wave, then reaches to push open the passenger door.

'Hi,' he says as I climb in, chucking my raincoat on the backseat.

'Hi.'

'Where are your parents?'

'Out at a meeting. They won't be back for a couple of hours.'

'So where are we going? You know the rivers are flooding?' He's turning the four-wheel drive around, heading out onto the road.

'Turn left,' I tell him, and he looks at me, wondering.

'We're not going back into town?'

'No.'

'Okay.'

I can tell he's disappointed, but he turns onto the road, heads left, windscreen-wipers going. He probably should have his lights on too, but I don't say anything. And he's wearing his leather boots and jeans with one of those large belt buckles. I just hope those boots are comfortable to walk in.

He's not asking about Pete's house either, not even looking back at what remains of it, or saying anything about the police tape still left there.

'You've been past here before, haven't you?' I ask him, realising.

'Do you think I wouldn't have been?'

I turn away, look out the window, don't know what to say. But then I have to talk, get him to turn off the Fairdown Straight onto Powerhouse Road. He slows for the railway crossing at the start of the road, looks both ways. It's uncontrolled, so no lights, no bells, no arm that comes down to stop the traffic. Over the tracks we wind up the narrow road past houses and life-stylers and farms. There are tall blue gums on one side of the road and near the end is a wooden-decked, single-lane bridge, the creek a raging torrent underneath it.

'Is this Deadmans?' Jack asks.

'It's Christmas Creek. It flows into Deadmans. We've got to stop here.'

He pulls over, off the side of the road before the bridge. Just before the set of locked gates.

'So what are we here for?'

'I thought we could go for a walk. You said you wanted to do something different, so how about a walk?'

'Where?'

'Up Mount Rochfort. There's a lake halfway up.'

'When I said I wanted to do something different together, I meant something out of the rain.'

'It won't be raining so much in the bush.'

'You're not convincing me.'

But he turns off the four-wheel drive and follows me anyway.

To start with, the path is not the easiest to find. We battle through manuka and then there it is, next to the flooding creek. There are tree ferns and taller trees, rimu and beech, and the track is mostly gravel, so not too muddy. I keep going, keep my head down, my hood pulled over my head, not saying much to Jack, hoping he will keep following. After about ten minutes I glance back and he's still there, looking around, looking at everything. It even seems like he might be enjoying it.

As the track leaves the bush by the creek it gets steeper until we are climbing along a ridge. Open country, scrubby yellow pine trees that were planted years ago but have never grown well because the soil is too poor, bracken fern and other plants I don't know the names of. Jack halts behind me and looks back, down the mountain. I stop too. You can just make out the line of Fairdown Beach through the rain. Somewhere in the distance there will be Cape Foulwind.

'Just don't go off the track, will you?' I tell him.

'Why?'

'There are mine shafts everywhere up here, all along the terraces. I don't know where exactly.'

'Mine shafts?'

'Old ones, from the eighteen hundreds. They go straight down. Most of them have got water in the bottom of them. You don't want to fall in. A farmer I know, Harry, he farms just over there,' I nod down the hill to our left, 'and he lost two of his dogs down one once. They were just running along in the fern and then they were gone. He had to go get a ladder to get them out.'

'Were they okay?'

'They were lucky. The shaft wasn't that deep.'

We're silent, looking again at what we can make out below us.

'It's a good walk,' Jack says. He's still catching his breath. 'I haven't had this much exercise for ages. Where does the road go?' He points to the gravel road that is snaking past us on the north side.

'That's the one that started from the locked gates where we parked. It goes up to the lake and then over towards Denniston. There used to be a power station with the lake, and they've got it going again. The water is piped down the mountain to turbines at the bottom. That's the access road to it all.'

'I'm guessing it would have been faster if we walked up the road?'

'Maybe. Not as nice though, and it's a private road. We shouldn't be on it.'

'And this track? Is it private too?'

'No, don't think so. But hardly anyone uses it. Want to keep going? We'll be back in the bush soon.'

'Sounds good,' he says, and follows me again.

We don't speak as the scrub gets higher and we climb off the ridge line and up a valley wall. We don't have the breath, and the rain is getting harder. We both want to get out of it, up into the trees again. Finally we're there, on the edge of the bush, and we stop, listening to the sound of the raindrops on the leaves above us.

I lower my hood, glance over at Jack. He still seems to be okay about what we're doing, even though he doesn't know why we're doing it. I'll have to tell him soon, I suppose. That is, if I'm right. I could be totally wrong, in which case I've ruined a perfectly good afternoon climbing a mountain when we could have been riding the horses on the beach.

I turn back to the track and start again. There are zigzags from here right to the lip of the lake and I climb up the first one.

'Annie, don't move.'

Jack's voice from behind me is suddenly mixed with panic, but I've already heard something in the ferns to my left, already felt it against my leg, already looked down, my eyes wide in disbelief, and seen the two black bootlaces tied together across the track. A tripwire.

'I'm not moving,' I say, trying to sound calm and failing badly.

Jack is pushing ferns aside on the right-hand side of the track, trying to see what the bootlaces are attached to.

'It's on the other side.' I point.

He swears when he sees it.

'It's Powergel, isn't it?' I ask.

'That's what it says on the wrapper.'

'Okay, there will be a detonator stuck into it and that will be wired to a battery. You've got to disconnect the battery, because that's the power source.'

'You sure? Can't you just take the tension off, move backwards?'

'I don't think so. I heard something click. I think I've already triggered it.'

'Okay, there's the battery. Stay still a second more.'

My leg feels like it's cramping up. I can't see what he's doing – the ferns are in the way, his body in the way.

'Okay, I've done it.'

'Show me.'

He holds up what looks to be a motorbike battery. I breathe and try to relax, try to move but nothing works. I reach down and grab the laces.

'Whoa, are you sure?' Jack says, seeing what I'm doing.

'It won't go off if there is no battery. It's fine.' I tug them out of the bush and then chuck them away. I collapse into the wet fern, trying to stop shaking.

'How do you know so much about Powergel?' he asks, tossing the battery.

'When your neighbour blows up his house with the stuff, you ask questions. My dad told me.'

'Because people in Westport know about this stuff.'

'It's just the way it is,' I manage to get out. I'm still having trouble breathing.

'You okay?' Jack asks me.

'That was kind of scary.'

'I think that's an understatement. That could have taken your legs off. Taken both of our legs off.'

'Or told someone that we're coming.'

'What do you mean?'

'Pete has put it there.'

'Pete? Your crazy neighbour who blew up his house?'

'I don't think he would have really wanted to hurt anyone, but maybe he put it there as some sort of alarm. A warning for him that someone was coming.'

'But it would hurt someone. It could have killed someone.'

'I don't think Pete always thinks things through like he should.'

'So what makes you think he's here?'

'I saw lights up this mountain last night.'

'This isn't some romantic walk in the bush in the rain, is it? This isn't you showing me a lake and a fantastic view from a mountain?'

'No. Is that what you thought it was?'

'Well, I was hoping.'

'Sorry. Are you angry?'

'Of course I'm angry. What were you thinking?'

'I had to do something.'

'But I'm also relieved you decided to bring me with you.' He's fishing his phone out of his pocket, making a call.

I sigh, look away, try to quieten my nerves, try to breathe so my heart rate slows down at least a bit. *Shit, Pete. Here I am trying to help you and you almost killed me. Booby-trap tripwires. What else is up this track?*

'No reception,' Jack says, frustrated, putting his phone back in his pocket.

'Were you trying to call your dad?'

'What do you think?'

'The cell phone tower is on top of the mountain. We're probably too tucked under it just here.'

'Now you tell me. So why do you believe Pete's up here?'

'He's been hiding out at Harry's farm.'

'The Harry with the farm dogs who fell down the mine shaft?'

'Yes. And with the police roadblocks and the rumours that they're going to start searching houses, I think it made Pete run.'

'And you know this how?'

'Remember, this is Westport. And Harry and his wife came to tea last night at our place, and I kind of guessed from the way they were acting.'

'Right, Westport again, where everyone knows everything but doesn't tell the people they should be telling. I get it. I suppose it was part of Dad's plan. Put the pressure on and something will happen. I don't think he was expecting this, though.' He stops, looks out at the rain thinking. 'If I decide to go back down, you're not coming with me, are you?'

'No.'

'And somehow I don't think I can stop you going up?'

'We might get phone reception higher up. And there is a lake to see.'

'I think keeping you safe is a better reason.' He sighs. 'Let's keep going if we have to do this. If you want to help him. I suppose it's okay to leave the Powergel there.'

'Well, I'm not carrying it with me.' I take his offered hand, hauling myself to my feet. I look up the zigzagging track, start off again. If it wasn't steep before, it is now.

'Just keep an eye out for anything,' Jack is saying behind me, already puffing.

'Like more booby-traps.'

'Like anything. The things I do for you.'

'Pete did save my life once.'

'Really?'

'I was five. I ran across the road after getting off the school bus and he stopped me.'

'So we're repaying a debt from ten years ago?'

'Kind of. But he's also our neighbour. He's not a bad guy.'

'I get it. It's okay.'

I don't know what to add to that, so I keep walking. Another ten minutes and we're finally at the top, the track levelling out, and my phone is vibrating in my pocket and it's not a text. Someone is ringing me. Sam, of all people.

'Hi, Sam,' I say. Jack stops, his eyes on me.

'Annie, Jack is your friend on Facebook,' Sam is saying in my ear. She doesn't sound too happy.

'Um, yes. So?'

'He liked a picture of Blue.'

'Did he?'

'Annie, you know him, don't you?'

'No.' I can't believe I'm discussing this. I almost just got killed by a tripwire and Sam wants to discuss Facebook friends.

'I know your Facebook policy – you only let people friend you who you know.'

'Okay, I know him. We've ridden together on the beach a few times. That's all.'

'You're his girlfriend, aren't you? The one he was talking about at the Cape Pub. He said he went riding with her on a beach. That she was amazing on a horse. That's you, isn't it?'

'I am not Jack's girlfriend.' Jack is still staring at me, but now he has his eyebrows raised. I'm not sure if he can hear Sam's side of the conversation, but I'm guessing he can, she's talking pretty loudly.

'You are his girlfriend,' Sam says, and I'm sure I can hear her crying. 'You're probably with him right now and you're just lying to me.'

'I'm not his girlfriend. I'll never be his girlfriend. He's already got one, and she is an amazing rider, so it's not me.'

'I don't believe you.' She ends the call before I get the chance to protest further.

'So we have phone coverage now?' Jack says slowly.

'Seems so.' I put my phone back in my pocket and start walking again.

'Just wait a minute. Who was that? Was it the girl from your class who I met?'

'Yes, it was Sam.'

'So?'

I stop, turn around. He hasn't moved. 'You liked a picture of Blue on my Facebook page and she must have seen it, so now she knows about us. Happy?'

'Sorry. I shouldn't have done that. I wasn't thinking.'

'Yeah, well, too late now.'

'So now she knows about us. But what's all this about you not being my girlfriend?'

'Well I'm not. Am I?'

'You're not?'

'No.'

'I just kiss you because, I don't know ... Why do I kiss you?'

'How would I know?'

'Maybe it's because I love you and that's why I tell you that all the time?'

'But you have a girlfriend.'

'Yeah – you.'

'So who's Stella, then? You know, the girl whose horse you ride?'

'What about Stella?'

'Your girlfriend Stella.'

'My girlfriend Stella? You think Stella is my girlfriend?'

'Isn't she? You miss her all the time and you ride her horse and your dad knows her and—'

'Annie, stop. Just stop. All this time you've been thinking Stella is my girlfriend?'

'Yes.'

'That's why … that's why everything? Why you keep me a secret, why there's this wall between us, this barrier I can't break through?'

He turns away. I don't know if he's angry or what. I do know I'm angry, and upset and confused, and I'm the one who should be angry, not him. How dare he kiss me and say all those things when Stella is so far away from him. Was he just going to hide everything from her, go back to normal when she gets back? He'll forget about me, I know that, but will she ever know? How many other girls has he kissed behind her back, when she's not there? All those girls on Facebook. Those thousands of girls on Facebook. He can have anyone he wants, whenever he wants. It's just not fair, nothing is fair. I brush away the tears from my face. I'm not going to let him see me cry. Not now, not ever again.

22

'Annie, Stella is not my girlfriend.' Jack's turned back around, is facing me. 'Stella is my sister.'

'What?'

'Stella is my younger sister. I thought you knew?'

'I don't believe you.'

'Annie ...'

'She's really your sister?'

'Yes. Annie, I'm so sorry. All this time, you thought ...' He's waiting for me. I can't say anything. I swallow. I stare at him.

'Annie, I love you. I go crazy when you're not around, when I can't see you. Annie – I – just listen to me, there is only you, just you. I hope there will always be just you.'

I nod. It's all I can do. Then he's holding me, and

wiping away the tears with his fingers and kissing me and for the first time, the first real time, I kiss him back. And we just hold each other, stand there, arms around each other, hearing each other's hearts beat. Then he lets me go, takes a step backwards.

'Okay?' he asks.

I take a deep breath. Nod.

He reaches out and smooths a strand of my wet hair behind my ear.

'I'd better call my dad, since we've got phone coverage here,' he says. 'Tell him what's happening, about the tripwire.'

'Do you have to? Can't we just find Pete, get him away?'

But Jack is already taking his phone out of his jacket pocket. 'It's going to voicemail,' he says after a minute, frowning. 'He must be busy.'

'Don't leave a message.'

He holds up his hand to quieten me. 'Hey Dad, it's me. Long story, but Annie thinks she knows where Pete is, the guy who blew up his house, and we're kind of walking up there. We're up at this place called Lake Rochfort, so if you could meet us up there that would be great. Take the road. You'll need boltcutters, there's a locked gate at the bottom. There was a tripwire on the walking track as you enter the bush again just before the lake so there could be more but …' He stops and sighs, ends the call, puts the phone back in his pocket. 'Lost the signal.' He shrugs. 'That's enough anyway. Aren't you going to try to ring your parents?'

'They'll still be in their meeting. No point. And anyway, what would I say? Please stop the police from somehow charging up here to arrest Pete?'

'Look, we'll find him, we'll tell him what's going on. Try to figure out how he's caught up in all of this.'

'And then what?'

'I don't know, but he can't stay up here hidden forever. Not with it raining like this. And he can't be putting trip-wires across paths where people walk.'

He points up the track and I start again, him following. We can glimpse the lake to our left now, grey in the rain. The bush is not as thick as it was in the zigzag. The trees are smaller, further apart. The walking is easier, which gives me time to think. Think about Pete, think about Jack, think about me. Me and Jack. Boyfriend, girlfriend. Me, having a boyfriend. Someone who loves me. Like really loves me. Maybe it's best not to think too much about it.

'Look, I'm sorry.' I've turned around to face Jack.

'Sorry for what?'

'For not realising, for not knowing about Stella, for thinking all that dumb stuff about you.'

'You don't have to be sorry. It's me who should be sorry, for not telling you about her. How many times have

I talked about her with you and I never told you she was my sister? It's my fault. I'm just glad that now you know. '

'Yes.'

'You do like me, you do want me as your boyfriend?'

'I've never had a boyfriend.'

'I'd figured that out. I've never had a girlfriend either, not a real girlfriend, if that helps.'

'But you've kissed other girls.'

'I kissed Sam in front of you, didn't I? You know it didn't mean anything.'

'I mean you've kissed girls the same way you kiss me.'

'No. Not like I kiss you.'

Silence. A fantail, in the bush next to us, at eye level, flits from bush to bush, its black tail feathers spread out.

'Annie, I've got to know. Do you feel the same way as I feel about you?'

I stay still, watching the fantail. Thinking. Thinking about us. Riding on the beach with him on Tassie, sitting in his four-wheel-drive, watching him on the school stage, talking to him on the phone, his dad, Stella. The boy in the black cowboy hat with calluses on his fingers. Jack Robertson, saddle bronc rider. Jack.

I nod.

'You've got to say it, you've got to tell me.' He's trying not to plead, trying not to be desperate, so I say it, what he wants to hear, just to please him. But suddenly I realise it's not about pleasing him, it's about being true to myself. It's about not hiding from the truth anymore.

'Yes. I love you.' And I reach out my hand and he holds it and smiles and looks away and then looks back at me and I know we're going to be okay. That everything is going to be okay. And we start walking again, but this time we're holding hands – the track just wide enough to allow us to do it.

'So how about all those Facebook photos of you and Stella?' I ask after a bit.

'What about them?'

'You've got your arms around her.'

'She's my sister, we hug. We're that type of family. What's wrong with that?'

'Just that—'

Below us, somewhere, down the mountain there's yelling. Then a noise, an explosion. Screaming.

'Another tripwire?' Jack asks.

'We would have seen it.'

'Is there more than one way to get up here?'

'There are tracks all through this bush.'

He's looking back down the track, his phone suddenly in his hand. 'No reception again.'

'Do you think your dad will have got your message by now?' My voice is shaking. I'm trying not to think about what must be happening down the track.

'No idea. But I don't think that would have been him. Even if he had got my message he wouldn't have had time to get here.'

'So who do you think it was? Who do you think is down there?'

'I don't know.'

The voices start up again, still loud, still shouting. I can't make out what they're saying. Just snatches, swearing. They're too far away.

'There's more than one of them,' Jack says. 'And they don't sound too happy. We'd better get going just in case. Run!'

Run? Run where? I don't have time to ask – Jack is already ahead of me on the track, following it as it curves in and out of the trees. He keeps glancing back, making sure I'm keeping up, and looking past me to see if anyone is following. I just hope he's looking out for tripwires too. I can't hear the shouting anymore. It's gone quiet. It's just the two of us, breathing hard. I'm looking back again when I almost crash into Jack. He must have suddenly stopped.

There, just off the track, is a man crouching in the ferns with a shotgun pointed right at us. Jack is slowly raising his arms, staring at him.

'Pete, what are you doing?' I call out, still puffing from the run. 'It's me, Annie, from across the road.' I bend over, my hands on my knees, trying to catch my breath, pull my raincoat hood off my head so he can see my face.

'Annie? What are you doing up here?'

'We're trying to find you.'

'I don't need finding. Who's this with you?'

'It's Jack,' I tell him.

Jack still has his arms raised, the gun still pointed at him.

'Jack Pearson from the fishing boats?'

'No. It's another Jack, you won't know him. He's from away. He's here to help too. Can you put the gun down?'

'Have you finally got a boyfriend, Annie?'

'Yes, he's my boyfriend.' I sigh, glancing across at Jack, who is almost grinning at what I've just said but also looking terrified. 'Put your arms down, it's okay,' I tell him.

'He has a gun pointed at me.'

'Pete, give it a rest, will you?'

Pete lowers the gun and stands up, pushes his long blond hair back from his face. He picks up another gun from by his feet and wades through the ferns to the track. He doesn't look like a guy who's been living rough for more than a week. He doesn't even have any stubble on his face. I wonder just how many of Di's scones he has eaten.

'You shouldn't be up here,' he says, looking Jack up and down, trying to figure him out. There must be only a couple of years' difference in ages between the two of them, but even a year makes a difference, especially, I suppose, when you're hiding from the police.

'There are people behind us,' Jack says. 'I don't know how many.'

'I know. You think I'm deaf or something? I heard the blast.'

'We have to get out of here.'

'It would be a good idea,' Pete says. 'You wouldn't know how to shoot a gun, would you?'

'One minute you're pointing it at me and now you're giving it to me?'

'Situations change, and if Annie likes you then you must be okay. So you know how to use one or not?'

'No.'

'Keep the pointy end away from anyone unless you want to kill them. The safety is here, see? It's on. There's a bullet up the spout, so be careful with it.' Pete hands Jack the gun. I can see now it's high calibre, something big. It's Harry's three-oh-three. Jack doesn't look at all comfortable holding it. 'If you're going to shoot someone, make sure you go for the chest. Easiest bit to hit. That'll take them down. If you be all silly about it and shoot them in the leg because you don't want to kill them, they'll just shoot you back. Okay? Go for the chest?'

Pete leads the way at a slow jog, sticking to the track. His leather boots are flopping on his feet, the laces missing.

Jack notices them too. 'No need to ask him who it was who set the tripwire,' he says.

I nod, thinking about what Harry had said about Pete. How he wouldn't hurt anyone. That it wasn't in him. *You got that one wrong, Harry.*

'Just keep that gun pointed away from me,' I tell him. 'You shouldn't trust the safety. There shouldn't be a bullet in the chamber, not when you're carrying it like this.'

'If you know so much about it then why didn't he give the gun to you?'

'Hurry up,' Pete calls back at us and we pick up the pace. A few minutes later, we're leaving the track, heading towards the shores of the lake. Jack is trying his phone again, the gun cradled against his chest.

'Nothing,' he tells me.

Somewhere, up above us in the cloud, is the cell phone tower on the top of Rochfort, but the angles must be all wrong again. We're glimpsing more of the lake through the trees now. The water is still, the grey surface only roughed up by the rain. I've never liked the look of it much. It's probably full of eels. The closer we get the more open the bush becomes, but even so, I don't see it until we're almost there. A corrugated iron shed. Pete is pulling the door open.

'Get in here,' he says and yanks the door shut behind us, then scoots down, his face up to the wall. There's a slit there in the iron, where two sheets don't quite meet.

A place to watch from, maybe to shoot from. 'Now sit down and keep quiet and let's see if I'm right about who's following us.'

We do what we're told, sitting on the dirt floor in the gloom. There are no windows, and with the door shut there's not a lot of light. At least it's dry, but there are enough possum and rat droppings everywhere for us to know we're not the only ones to use it. A tramping pack is against one wall. It's full and ready to go, straps done up. While I've been looking around Jack has found another hole in the iron, about half a metre off the ground, and he's lying stretched out, the gun ready, peering out of it.

'Just don't shoot unless we have to,' Pete is telling him over the noise of the rain on the roof. 'If they walk right past us, all the better. Then we'll have the jump on them.'

I crawl up next to Jack, to see if I can look out of the hole as well. He's loosening then tightening his hands on the gun, but they're still shaking. He doesn't want to go along with Pete's plan and nor do I but I don't think either of us have got any choice. I lean over and push the safety off, and Jack glances back at me.

'I've used this gun,' I explain. 'It pulls slightly to the left.'

'You've used this gun?'

'It belongs to Harry.'

'The farmer with the dogs? Pete's stolen it?'

'I think Harry probably gave it to him.'

'I'm not going to even ask why. So how come you've used it?'

'I shot a deer with it once, not far from here.'

Jack shakes his head at me in disbelief again. 'You take it.' He hands me the gun and rolls away.

Pete doesn't say anything, so I shuffle to where Jack was lying, look out the hole. Nothing to see but ferns, the track further on. Trees. Rain. Not that I want to see anything else. I'm scared, just like Jack. Except it was my idea to come up here. I got him into this.

'Who are these people?' Jack calls softly over to Pete.

'Just people,' Pete says. 'So, Annie, who told you I was up here?'

'No one. I overheard Harry talking to you on the phone last night.'

'When they were around at your place for tea?'

'Later I saw lights up here. It wasn't hard to figure it out.'

'You shouldn't have come. You both shouldn't have come. I don't need saving.'

'I wasn't really given the option,' Jack mutters.

I look back through the gap in the iron, wondering what to say. Maybe nothing. Jack's right. I should have told him everything, before we started up the mountain. It was just all this girlfriend stuff. If I had known about Stella, if I had known he was serious when he kissed me, that he wasn't just fooling around like I thought he was, then maybe I would have been more honest with him. I mumble something about being sorry.

Everyone is silent again, waiting, watching, listening. Just the sound of the rain on the roof. Which is good. That's all I want to hear. I don't want to hear footsteps, large or small. A pile of rat droppings is right by my hand and the last thing I want to see right now is a rat, or anything.

But Jack is still thinking. When I glance at him I can see it. He's frowning, working things through in his head. It makes him look like his dad, a much younger version. Maybe that's what he's doing – figuring out the stuff that his dad would be figuring out right now, if he was here, like how we're all going to get out of this alive. I hope that's what he's thinking about.

'So, Pete,' Jack is asking.

'What?'

'How come these other people know you're up here?'

'Because I invited them up,' Pete says.

I glance over at Pete, wondering. He's sitting by the wall, calmly staring through the slit, the shotgun on the ground, his hand on it ready.

'You did what?' I whisper.

'They killed my mate. It's time for payback.'

23

'The body in the Orowaiti River, the one that ended up on the beach?' I say slowly.

'His name was Ben.'

I glance at Jack. He nods back. The name would have been in the papers, online, but I haven't been following it. Not in the past few days. Not with the possibility of Dad losing his job. But Jack would have known it. He closes his eyes for a second and I know now exactly what he's thinking. How did he get to be holed up in a tin shed in the middle of nowhere, where there is no cell phone coverage, with a crazy guy who wants to kill people who no doubt want to kill him first? Less than two hours ago he was picking up his girlfriend from her house hoping to take her out for a coffee in a warm café. Where did he go wrong?

'Ben used to work up the hill at Stockton,' Pete is saying. 'He used to set the explosives, to take the overburden off. Then in the last round of layoffs, he got the chop. Anyway, about a month ago these guys came up to Ben and me in the pub. They were truck drivers who'd worked with Ben at the mine, they knew what he could do. They'd all been laid off, just like him. But they were a lot older than us. Had families. They needed money, so they had this plan to rob banks over in Christchurch.'

'So what happened?' Jack asks.

'We thought it was all rot. Pub talk. But we went along with it for a laugh. See what would happen. We had nothing else to do anyway. Ben showed them how to wire stuff up, use blasting caps, timers, everything. We were just having fun. Like when we were kids and we used to pull firecrackers apart.'

'Where did they get them from? The explosives?'

'We didn't know. They just had a few, nothing much, nothing that would really cause any damage. Maybe take your hand off if you weren't careful. That's why we weren't really worried or anything. Then one night they showed us all this stuff they had stolen from the shed out on the pakihi.'

'Powergel. And you realised then they weren't joking.'

'Ben got scared and tried to tell them that we weren't interested, so they hit him and he fell and he just didn't get up again. They made me help them dump him in the Orowaiti River and then everything went to shit.'

'So why not just go to the police?'

'I wanted to, but they would have started accusing me of doing drugs or something. I mean, I smoke a bit of weed but so does everyone around here. Then I got drunk and went around to the cop shop anyway but there was no one there, or so I thought. It was all dark. Shut up. No one answered. So I went nuts and shot a few things I probably shouldn't have.'

'Like the police station,' Jack says.

'I know. Dumb, real dumb. I was just drunk and angry and I wanted to talk to someone. I didn't even know anyone had heard or seen me until I realised the police had surrounded my house the next morning. So then I had to come up with a plan.'

'What was the plan?' Jack asks.

'I blew up Mum's house, so everyone would think I was dead. Hey, Annie, thanks for those sandwiches, by the way.'

'No problem,' I say, avoiding Jack's glance.

'They were really good sandwiches. Anyway, I made it out onto the beach the next day and headed for Harry's farm. He's always helped me in the past, and I've been holing up there. Found out the police figured I wasn't in the house when I blew it up, so that plan failed. When I heard they were going to start searching places I couldn't let Harry and Di get in trouble, so I hoofed it up here. Really, I just want it to be all over. I just want to do normal stuff again. Go to the pub. You know. It's not like I've done anything wrong. Not when you think about it.'

I hope Jack is not going to make a comment on this last bit. He's still staring at me. Maybe he's working out why I really was on the beach that day with Blue when we first met, and whether he wants to have a criminal as a girlfriend. Whether he'll come and visit me in prison. I'm still not sure what he thinks about me shooting a deer. Ever since I took the gun from him he's been looking at me weirdly.

'So do these men know about this place, this hut?' Jack asks Pete, switching his attention from me.

'No. Shouldn't, I don't think.'

'But you said you invited them up here. How?'

'I phoned one of them, used Harry's phone. Told them I was coming up here.'

'Because?' The way Jack asks it I can tell he's not at all happy.

'As I said, I want it over with.'

'So your intention is just to kill them all?'

'Don't know. If I have to. I've already taken at least one of them out with that tripwire on the track. That was my doorbell. So I knew they were coming.'

'It could have been anyone walking up the mountain. It was almost us.' Jack is still whispering, still keeping his

192

voice down. He can just be heard above the sound of the rain, but he's getting angry. Scared and angry.

'You guys weren't meant to be up here. No one comes up here. I didn't invite you.'

'So what was your plan? The tripwire tells you they're coming, then you scurry in here to see what happens next?'

'I was going shoot them in the bush. They wouldn't have known what hit them.'

'So what are we doing in this shed, then?'

'You guys stuffed it up, didn't you? Now we'll just have to take them out from here. More cover for three people than a fern or something. I should see them first, so I'll get the first shots in and anyone I miss, you get, Annie. You okay with that?'

'Suppose so,' I say, trying to keep my voice level. I'm feeling sick inside, wishing like anything I hadn't come up here looking for Pete. That I hadn't brought Jack with me. What if I have to shoot someone, like Pete wants me to? Like really shoot someone, before they shoot us? It was hard enough shooting that deer. It was just because Dad was there that I managed to do it, because Harry was talking quietly in my ear, looking down the barrel of the gun with me, telling me exactly what to do, what to expect. When I finally saw the dead animal up close I didn't know what to think. Here was this beautiful creature, lying in the bush, and I had killed it. There was the hole in its side, blood, the eyes still open, still clear. Minutes ago it was crashing through the trees and now it was stopped forever. Because of me.

'Hey, Annie,' Pete's saying, 'you look pretty good lying there with that gun, you know. You look like you could take out a whole army.'

Now I'm really avoiding Jack's stare and I'm hoping like crazy he doesn't take Pete's compliment the wrong way, that Pete's eyeing up his girlfriend. And I don't want to take out an army, I don't want to take out anyone, and lying here on the dirt in my raincoat, my hair still dripping wet, my heart beating so fast in my chest that it hurts, I doubt I look pretty good to anyone.

But I don't get the chance to say anything back to Pete because noise erupts on the far side of the shed. Something hard is raked across the corrugated iron outside, deafening us, and the door bursts open.

I struggle up, swing the gun around, but I'm not fast enough. It's kicked out of my hands. Jack is somehow on his feet yelling and so is Pete and he's swinging the shotgun everywhere and the shed is suddenly crowded. I'm reaching for the gun on the ground but the same guy kicks me this time, in the side, and I slam against the wall, screaming in pain, in fear.

'Don't hurt her,' Jack is yelling and he tries to punch the guy but the guy just hits him with his gun and Jack goes down and then I'm screaming again and the men are yelling and Pete is swearing and threatening to shoot them all.

'Just shut up, will you, all of you,' a man shouts above us and then there's just the sound of the rain, hitting the iron roof. It's started to bucket down outside. Four men are standing in the shed, guns pointed at us, one of them is Harry's three-oh-three. Jack is crouched on the ground, shaking, a gun in his face. Pete is pinned next to the door, the shotgun still in his hands.

'Just put it down, Pete, don't be stupid,' the man says.

Pete stares up at him and for a second I think he's not going to do what the man wants. His finger is on the shotgun's trigger. If there were more distance, maybe he could take out two of them with the shot, but this close there's no way.

Maybe he has got a death wish, maybe he doesn't care if he goes down in a hail of bullets, but I care. I don't want to see him die, not like this. And if they shoot Pete, what will they do to us?

'Put it down, Pete,' the man says again and Pete's hand starts to relax. 'Put it down slowly now.' Pete at last lays the gun on the ground and hesitantly stands up. One of the other men reaches down and grabs the gun.

'So I see you've got some new mates, Pete,' one of the other men says over the noise of the rain on the roof.

'They're just kids,' the one who picked up the guns says.

The first one, the one with the deep voice, is staring at me. I'm holding my side, my ribs still aching from his kick.

'I know you,' he says. 'I know your dad. He drives the trains, doesn't he?'

I glance up at him. I don't recognise him at all. The men are wearing raincoats and waterproof leggings. One of them, the one who kicked me, has a beanie on. They look like ordinary men, men I could pass walking down the main street and never think anything about, except they all have guns and they're pointing those guns at us.

'So what are we going to do?' the one with the beanie says.

'Do what we planned to do, it's just there'll be three bodies instead of one. Could fit a hundred bodies down that old mine shaft and you still wouldn't find them.'

'This is getting out of hand,' says the one with the deeper voice, the one who knows Dad.

'He started it. He put that booby-trap on the track. He's probably killed Doug.'

'Doug should have been looking where he was going. They're just kids.'

'Too late.'

'But I know Annie.'

'Tough.'

I glance over at Pete. He has his head down, his hair covering his eyes. Jack is looking over at me. He's scared, really scared. The grey light from the open door has him framed against the wall, like an animal caught in a car's headlights. The heavy rain has suddenly slackened off again, leaving as fast as it came, but it's still falling, the water forming a curtain across the doorway.

I try to think of something to say, like *don't shoot us* or *let us go and we won't tell anyone* but it all sounds like some crappy movie in my head. I want to plead for my life, for Jack's life, for Pete, but I don't know how to. I need a convincing argument, a persuasive reason, like my English assignment was meant to have. The fact that I suck at English is going to get us all killed because I can't think of the right words. It's just stupid and crazy and I don't want to die like this, I don't want Jack and Pete to die like this.

'Get up, all of you. Now,' the man with the beanie shouts at us.

I force myself up against the wall, the metal cold and damp against my hands. Someone is pushing me towards the doorway. I'm stumbling, but a hand grabs me and I manage to keep on my feet and then I'm out into the rain.

'Start walking,' the man says.

24

'Watch where you put your feet,' Pete mutters as he pushes past me to take the lead.

'Hey, not you,' one of the men yells. 'The girl goes first.'

The rain is falling on my face, waking me up, making me feel stronger, braver, even though my ribs are still hurting like anything. I don't think anything is broken; at least I hope nothing is broken. I turn and give the man the coldest stare I can, then set off down the track, Jack right behind me. Pete obediently waits for us, standing in the fern.

I'm thinking about what Pete said. This is not the way he led us to the hut, not the direction the men came from, otherwise we would have seen them. This is where Pete had been looking out of the slit in the shed wall. He was looking this way for a reason. This is the way he was hoping they would come. I watch where I put my feet and hope Jack will do the same behind me, try to ignore the pain in my ribs from where the guy kicked me.

And then I see it. He's used what looks like the drawstring from the top of the tramping pack this time. A black cord stretched limply across the track, the ends hidden in ferns on either side.

I step over it, careful that I don't touch it, but even more careful that the men following don't see me do it. Nothing. I keep walking, holding my breath, listening to Jack's footsteps behind me, hoping he's seen it too. *How much explosive did you use with this one, Pete? Enough to blow us all up?* Jack must have stepped over it. I breathe again. Now there will be Pete. At least he will know it's there.

I'm not looking back; I'm too scared to look back. Now we're all over it safely I lengthen my stride, trying to give us all more space, to get ready to run, my heart already beating fast enough for me to run a marathon. Even my fingers are tingling. I try to breathe slowly. In and out, in and out. Another step, and another, further and further away from it. Just keep going. Just keep breathing.

The explosion is like a starter's gun. I'm leaping forward before I even realise what's happening, the blast pushing me. My first stagger becomes a stride and then I'm running as hard as I can through the trees, jumping the ferns, not looking back. My ears are ringing with the sound of the explosion, of gunfire, yells, screams, wood splintering next to me as a bullet lands in a tree trunk. Jack is behind me, breathing hard, his legs crashing through the undergrowth. I catch sight of Pete way over to my left, dodging the gunfire between the trees. I start doing the same, weaving this way and that, keeping moving, making myself a harder target to hit. Getting further and further away.

The lake is still on our right but we've lost the track completely, run past where it zigzags down through the tall trees. The bush is thicker here. We're pushing through branches, fighting our way under when we otherwise can't get through. There are fallen logs, holes, gullies. A bank stops me for a second. I have to scramble up it but Jack grabs me.

'Quiet,' he whispers in my ear. We stay like that, buried in the fern against the bank, listening, our hearts both racing.

There's nothing.

'Have we …?' I whisper.

'I don't know.'

We stay still for another minute, then another, and still nothing. Just the sound of the rain falling on the bush above us, dripping through the leaves.

'Let's keep going but stay down, as quiet as we can,' he says, and I move again, crawl up the bank. I can just make out a path made by a deer, or some sort of animal. It will be easier going if we follow it, quieter.

'Annie, wait.'

'What?' I turn around.

'Just stop. There's blood. Is that you?'

I stare down at where he's pointing and see the blood on the fern I've just crawled through. Bright red. The rain washing it off already. And then I notice the hole in my raincoat.

Almost out of curiosity I touch it. It's tiny. So tiny. I look up at Jack and he's seen it too, his face going pale even as I watch.

'Annie?' He's ripping open my raincoat, the domes, fumbling with the zip, pushing up my clothes from my waist, and I'm feeling sick and scared and suddenly I can't stand up anymore and Jack has me and he's got my raincoat off and I'm on the ground, on the path, and the rain is falling on my face and I can smell the bush all around me, the deep peaty smell of leaves and rain and ferns and moss. And it's got cold, so cold.

Soon it will be dark and we're wet and cold and we need to get out of the rain. We need to get somewhere warm and I'm telling Jack this but he's not listening. We have to move. We have to get somewhere warm. Why won't he listen to me? Instead he's grabbing me again, rolling me over, pushing up my clothes.

'The bullet's gone right through.'

He lies me down in the moss and the ferns and I look up at him. He's trying his phone and I wish he would hurry up because I'm getting really cold now. So cold. Just so cold. I close my eyes.

There are noises, someone running, pushing through the undergrowth towards us. I can feel the footsteps through the ground. Jack is grabbing me, trying to pull me off the path, but it hurts.

'Pete? Is that you?' he calls out quietly.

'What are you doing? We've got to get out of here,' Pete says. He's puffing.

'Annie's been shot.'

'Is she going to be okay?'

Jack doesn't reply. I'm listening for a reply, waiting for a reply, but instead they're picking me up, both of them, carrying me somewhere. Further into the bush. Then Pete's hands are searching my body, his breath on my face.

'You got to stop the bleeding, mate,' he's saying. 'And she's cold. She's really cold. You've got to do something.'

'I don't know what to do.'

'She's going to die out here. Annie and I—' He stops, about to say something, then changes his mind. 'You can't let her die.'

'I don't know what to do.'

'Here, hold this against it, stop the bleeding.'

Pressure against my side, something soft pressed against where the pain is. I gasp.

'It's hurting her.'

'Just do it.'

'I can't get hold of my dad, there's no cell phone coverage here.'

'What do you want get hold of your dad for? How is he going to help you?'

'He's a cop.'

'Now you tell me.'

'You have to help us. Please.'

'What sort of cop? Like a cop who can get a helicopter here with some firepower?'

'Yes.'

'Lots of firepower?'

'Yes. He's lead detective on your case. He's Detective Inspector Grant Robertson.'

'Give me your phone. Where's the number? Is it under "D" for "dad"?'

'Yes. Here it is. Password is two thousand.'

'You stay with Annie and I'll look for some coverage. Then I'll have to go so the cops don't find me. Which means you have to look after Annie. You keep the pressure on and you keep her warm and you don't let her die She's my neighbour. You don't let her die. Okay?'

'Okay.'

More noise, rustling in the ferns, and then he's gone. Silence. Then a sob. Jack. I reach up my hand, grab his arm.

'You're going to be fine, Annie,' he says after a bit. 'Pete's gone to get help.' His voice sounds calm, steady. 'How about we get you a little warmer? I'll just try not to hurt you.' I hear his jacket unzipping and then feel him pulling me up beside him, into his arms, across his body, pushing my raincoat over until it covers us both like a blanket. I feel his warmth through my back. Feel his heart beat, his chest rise and fall underneath me.

'You're like ice,' he says. 'Hey, talk to me, Annie. Don't go to sleep on me. Annie?' Then he swears. 'Hurry up, Pete,' he says, and then I must have gone to sleep or something because suddenly there are voices. Loud voices. I open my eyes. Jack is still holding me. He hasn't moved, but it's dark. There are torch beams flashing through the trees. When did it get dark?

'Hey, look at this,' one of the voices is saying. It's a man, a deep voice. I remember that voice.

'That's blood. I thought we'd shot one of them.' A different voice, lighter. 'Where's it going?'

'I don't know. The rain has washed most of it away.' The voice of the man who knows me.

'They could be close.'

'They could be anywhere. We should keep going.'

I look up at Jack. I can just make him out in the blackness. He's listening, watching the torch beams. He sees my eyes are open and puts his finger to his lips, signalling *keep quiet, keep still*. I nod, close my eyes again. The sound of the men drifts off. The one who knows me leading them away.

Somehow I fall back asleep. Dream. I dream of riding Tassie down Fairdown Beach at full gallop, bareback, no saddle, no bridle, nothing. It's raining and there's water streaming off us, off her black coat and my raincoat and then we're not galloping but swimming, swimming through dark blue water but we're under the water, deep, and we're not breathing, we can't breathe, we don't have to breathe, we're just swimming, Tassie strong underneath me, her legs pushing through the water and it's dark and cold and wet but she keeps swimming and I keep holding on, my legs pressed against her side, my coat undone, swept back in the water, Tassie's tail streaming behind us, my fingers wrapped tightly in her mane. And I know I'm not going to let go.

Tassie.

25

There is a hand curled around mine, next to me, on the bed. Calluses on the fingers, on the palm.

◆ ◆ ◆

I wake again and this time there are voices. Raised voices. My dad's, then Mum's, then Dad's again. The hand with the calluses is still holding mine but tighter now. I squeeze it back.

◆ ◆ ◆

This time I open my eyes. It's dark, half-dark, light coming in from a corridor, from machines, displays by my bed. Jack is sitting in a chair, his head on the sheet next to my thigh, one of his hands still holding mine. He's asleep.

I do an inventory, wiggle my toes, turn my head on the pillow to look at the lines and wires going from my body to the machines. I'm warm, I'm dry, I'm clean. I can't smell anything but hospital. I lick my lips. Stretch out one leg, then the other. Wriggle my toes again. Lift my head. Everything works. I'm alive.

A nurse slips in through the half-open door and takes a chart off the end of the bed and looks up at me.

'You're awake,' she whispers.

I nod back, wide-eyed.

'How are you feeling? Any pain?'

'I'm okay.' My voice sounds raspy, my throat dry.

'Here, drink this.' She takes a glass of water with one of those bendy straws from a table. She holds the straw between my lips. The water has ice in it.

'Thanks,' I say, as she puts the glass back on the table. She starts reading the file, checking the displays, writing things down.

'I've just got to take your temperature.' She holds a thing in my ear, checks it and writes something. 'You're doing fine. We'll have you up for a shower tomorrow morning.'

I nod back.

'You know you're in Christchurch Hospital? They brought you in by chopper.'

'I don't remember.'

'People pay a lot of money for a trip in a helicopter over the alps and you did it for free and don't remember a thing.' She sighs. 'Always the way.'

Jack stirs in his sleep and the nurse glances over at him.

'He's hardly left your side, you know,' she whispers. 'Your parents aren't very impressed, by the way, but your grandmother likes him.' She smiles. 'Most of the nursing staff like him too. We're not meant to let people stay after visiting hours, but you two are different. It's been all over the news what you two did up that mountain. You're both heroes. And he saved your life, so we think he can stay. Now how about you get some more sleep?'

♦ ♦ ♦

When I wake again it's morning and I'm alone. Sun is coming in through the window, noise coming from the corridor, clattering and banging and people walking up and down and voices. A breakfast tray is on the table at the end of my bed, just toast crumbs left on the plate, an empty glass. Past that, at the end of the room, I see a shelf with vases of flowers. Too many to count. And get-well cards.

Jack's dad walks in and looks around. He's in a suit, wearing a tie this time, a takeaway coffee in one hand.

'Sorry, I thought Jack would be here,' he says. 'Do you know where's he gone?'

I shake my head. Stare at him.

'You must be feeling better, eating breakfast,' he says, putting the coffee next to the tray and taking my chart from the end of my bed. He looks at it, like he understands what he's reading.

Then Jack is there, a toothbrush in his hand, a towel around his neck, dressed in a T-shirt and jeans.

'You're awake?' he says, startled. 'I duck out for five minutes and you wake up?'

But I can't answer. All I can do is cry and he has his arms around me, his face pressed against mine, and we stay like that, holding each other as everything that happened floods back into my head. The explosions, the gunshots, the blood, the helicopter, the sirens of the police cars driving up the road towards the lake. I remember the helicopter now. The sound of it echoing against the mountain as it came closer to us. The noise of the rotors, more shots, screaming. The lights in the darkness. Then the silence. The voice of Jack's dad calling out Jack's name, calling out my name.

'Hey, it's okay. It's over,' Jack says in my ear. 'It's all over. They caught them all.'

And he holds me away from him and looks at me, and I try to smile but I can't stop crying.

'The pain relief she's on,' his dad says from the other side of the room, 'it will make her emotional.'

209

I almost laugh but I'm sore, my side is so sore. Even breathing makes it hurt.

'And she's about due for some more, so just be careful how you hold her.'

'Did you eat my breakfast?' I manage to ask Jack, wiping the tears from my face.

'I can get you another one, I think. Are you hungry?'

'Maybe later.'

He hands me a tissue he's found somewhere, puts some pillows behind me, raises the head of the bed with some device. 'Comfortable?'

'Thanks.'

Jack's dad puts the chart back where it belongs.

'Now you're awake we'll have to get a statement from you about what happened,' he says to me. 'Maybe later today?'

I nod.

'Pete's fine, by the way. It took us a while to find him up that mountain. He's going to have to do some prison time – even though he believes he's innocent of every crime he's ever committed. Apparently he thinks it is acceptable behaviour to blow up a house in Westport, if you own it yourself. But what he did up there to save you both, rest assured it will be taken into account.'

'Thank you,' I tell him. Jack is still fussing with the pillows.

'And I hear from your parents that we'll be seeing a lot more of you. With your dad losing his job and all of you moving to Christchurch. Jack tells me you're not too bad on Tassie, so if you could help out exercising the other horses, Jack may be able to find room for Blue in our stables here at no cost.'

I nod again. It's all I can do.

'Jack,' he says, and Jack finally turns to his father. 'Jack, I've got to go, but one word: schoolwork please. Well, that's two words, but get some done, okay?'

'See you later, Dad,' Jack says. The look on his face says it all – *Dad, just get lost, now.*

◆ ◆ ◆

The sun has come out, although it might only be brief. The last few weeks have been fine while we packed up the house, but last night it rained, with more forecasted. Jack drove Tassie over with him yesterday from Christchurch and we had one final ride on Fairdown Beach in the afternoon. Even he admitted it wasn't the same in the sunshine, that he missed the rain. It felt good to be riding again, my stomach only aching slightly from where the bullet went in. Jack lifted up my T-shirt to inspect the wound, pressing his fingers against it. 'You're going to be left with a scar,' he whispered.

But that was yesterday and now everything is dripping wet again and glistening and Blue has to leave. We're hoping it will settle Blue, having Tassie for company for the four-hour drive through the alps. Jack has backed the float down our driveway, past the real estate agent's *Sold* sign by our hedge. A retired couple from Nelson have bought the house. They didn't want to live in a city, and they loved the look of our home, how old it was – and the freshly painted pale blue hallway, of course.

So now I'm standing with Blue, one hand holding his lead rope, the other on his halter, Mum and Dad watching. Dad starts his new job on Monday, still driving trains, but along the East Coast out of Christchurch this time. There won't be shift work, and he won't have to work through the night, so he's happy. And Mum is happy, although she hasn't found a job yet. She'll start looking once we are all settled. The school was sad to see her go.

Jack has given me one chance to get Blue onto the float, and if it doesn't work he'll do it himself.

I've told Blue what's about to happen, when we were alone and no one else was listening. That this is goodbye to his paddock, to the beach, to Westport, to the Coast, to the rain. He listened, stamped his feet, ate his hay. I don't think he understood. How could he? I don't even think I do.

And this is it. Right now. A few steps, that's all it will take, and he will be on the float and the door will be shut and he and Jack and Tassie will be on the road to Christchurch. I tighten my hand around the halter strap.

I take a deep breath. 'Okay, Blue, let's do this.'

I wish he would take one last look at his paddock, at the bush, at the mountains, at the sky. But he doesn't. He just munches on the carrot he found in my pocket, the one I was meant to use to lead him into the float. I step forward and he moves with me. I'm up onto the ramp of the float, Blue right beside me, but then his front hooves hit the metal and the sound echoes against the inside of the box and there he stops. I let go of his halter and keep walking into the float, pulling on the lead rope, but I know it's no use. He has his back heels dug in. He's not going anywhere. Tassie, in her stall, looks back at us bored.

Jack takes the lead rope out of my hands and turns Blue around, off the ramp. He walks him around our driveway for a minute and then walks straight back onto the float and inside. Blue follows without a misstep. Then Jack is back out, closing the doors.

'He's fine,' he tells me.

'You sure?'

'He'll be fine. I promise.' Then Jack looks around, makes sure my parents aren't watching, and kisses me.

'See you over there,' he says.

AUTHOR'S NOTE

In 2012, about 1100 people were employed at Solid Energy's Stockton open-cast mine but only three years later it had dropped to 225 as coal exports to China and elsewhere dwindled and the price of coal fell. The lower volumes of coal transported by rail to Lyttelton meant train drivers lost their jobs too. Government-owned Solid Energy had invested heavily in expansion before the Global Financial Crisis and could no longer pay its interest bill so the mine was put on the market in 2015, which is when this book is set. In early 2016, Solid Energy announced that a decision on whether to close Stockton, if it was not sold, would be made by mid-year. At the last minute it was bought by a group of businesses that have ties to Westport. They took over the mine in 2017.

Further south, Spring Creek near Greymouth, also owned by Solid Energy, was not so lucky. It failed to find a buyer and the mine was sealed and flooded in 2017/2018. It was believed to be the last underground coalmine in the country.

New Zealand coalmines are not the only ones to have closed, or partly closed, around the world. In December 2015, Britain's very last underground coalminers came topside for the final time at the Kellingley mine in North Yorkshire. In Australia, Queensland's Isaac Plains, a coking coalmine like Stockton, sold for just $1 in 2015. Three years earlier it had been valued at $A860 million. More than 4000 coalmining jobs were lost in Australia between 2014 and 2016. Mines have closed and jobs lost also in the United States – in West Virginia, Kentucky, Colorado, Indiana and Utah.

ACKNOWLEDGEMENTS

I've got to thank amazing author Stacy Gregg who I met at a Storylines event in Dunedin in 2015. She reminded me just how good horse stories are. It's because of her that Annie has Blue in this book. Stacy, I hope I got all of the horse stuff right! And also my thanks to Jan and Ian MacKenzie, Wayne and Bronwyn Smaill, and Colin and Barbara Chalmers, for also answering all my questions about pacers and quarter horses and barrel racing and saddles and bridles and everything else I needed to know about horses. Thanks guys. Now we can talk about other stuff, like cows and sheep and tractors.

Thank you to all of the good friends we have in Westport – the Jacksons, O'Connors, Hamiltons, Parsons, Milnes, Keoghans and Coburns, who we can always call in on at any time and they always welcome us home.

Thank you to M for taking me and the rest of my family on that trip through the Buller River Gorge many years ago – not on the road side.

Thank you to the fantastic team at Allen & Unwin in Melbourne, Sydney and Auckland. Without you this story wouldn't be told. Thank you to Eva, Susannah, Hilary, Sophie, Angela, Julia, Jo and everyone else who has been involved. Thank you also to my amazing agent Grace Heifetz at Curtis Brown Australia.

Thank you to John McIntyre of the Wellington Children's Bookshop, who told me he wanted so much to read this book, especially as he had grown up at Jacksons near Otira on the West Coast. John, we were so lucky to have you. We miss you.

And thank you to Country Blue, who I once galloped down Fairdown Beach, totally out of control, until we had to stop at the mouth of Whareatea River. And I didn't fall off.